D0648484

Take Care of My Girl

PATRICIA HERMES

Take Care of My Girl

A NOVEL

210 5864

REMOVED FROM COLLECTION

Little, Brown and Company
Boston   Toronto   London

WEST ISLIP PUBLIC LIBRARY
3 HIGBIE LANE
WEST ISLIP, NEW YORK 11795

Copyright © 1992 by Patricia Hermes

All rights reserved. No part of this book may be reproduced in
any form or by any electronic or mechanical means, including
information storage and retrieval systems, without permission
in writing from the publisher, except by a reviewer who may
quote brief passages in a review.

First Edition

The characters and events in this book are fictitious. Any
similarity to real persons, living or dead, is coincidental and
not intended by the author.

Library of Congress Cataloging-in-Publication Data ·
Hermes, Patricia.
Take care of my girl : a novel / by Patricia Hermes. — 1st ed.
  p.   cm.
Summary: A school project propels Brady Abbot and her grandfather
on a search for her father, who left them six years earlier.
  ISBN 0-316-35913-0
  [1. Family life — Fiction.   2.Grandfathers — Fiction.   3. Fathers
and daughters — Fiction.]   I. Title.
PZ7.H4317Tak   1992
[Fic] — dc20   92-9819

10 9 8 7 6 5 4 3 2 1

RRD-VA

Published simultaneously in Canada
by Little, Brown & Company (Canada) Limited

Printed in the United States of America

*For my son, Tim,
and his Angel*

Take Care of My Girl

Chapter 1

"Hey, watch this!" I said to Danielle. "You ought to try it."

I was lying on my back on Danielle's bed, letting my gerbils, Peanut Butter and Jelly, run up and down all over me. Danielle had been keeping them for a while because my neighbors had just gotten a new cat, Roxy — and Roxy kept coming to my house and eyeing my gerbils as if she thought they were cat food. They'd be safe for a while at Danielle's till I trained Roxy. Besides, Danielle loves gerbils and isn't allowed to have her own. Her mother says *gerbil* is just a fancy name for a rat.

I lifted Jelly up and put her on my face.

"Brady! Stop!" Danielle said. "She's going to poop on your face."

I turned Jelly around and headed her back toward my stomach again.

"Listen, Brady," Danielle said, "you've got to be extra careful now, with gerbils and with Roxy and

3

everything else. Our horoscopes say trouble, big time!"

She was sitting cross-legged beside me on the bed, and she pointed to the horoscope she was reading in the newspaper.

Danielle is always reading horoscopes — horoscope books, newspaper horoscopes, even the horoscopes that are printed on bubble gum wrappers. And the more bizarre the predictions, the more she likes it.

I pretended I hadn't heard. It's best to ignore Danielle's horoscopes, or else she gets really wacky.

Danielle looked over at me. "Okay," she said. "So ignore me. You'll be sorry." She bent over the paper. "Just listen to this: 'The stars are in a most unfavorable configuration for you right now. This could spell considerable trouble for you in upcoming days. Keep your affairs in good order.' " She looked up. "It could mean your Save the Earth project is in trouble at school. It could mean some trouble with bratty Michele. It could even be Fishface up to something. But trouble!"

I tried to keep a straight face. "It could even mean the end of the world," I said.

Danielle flopped back on the bed and tossed the newspaper on the floor. "Funny," she said.

"And don't throw away that newspaper!" I said.

"I'm not, I'm not!" she said.

"Yeah," I said. "But you forget sometimes. You know what would happen if everyone in the United States recycled their Sunday newspaper every week?"

Danielle rolled her eyes. "You've told me a zillion

4

times: We could save five hundred thousand trees a week!"

I grinned. I had taught her well.

But I thought I heard her mutter something like, "Big deal!"

She looked over at me. "So don't believe in the stars. But they know. They predict the future."

"Wrong," I said. "No way a star can predict trouble."

But I held my gerbils a little tighter. Sometimes, it seems like Danielle does know when something bad's going to happen — like last summer, when she said we were going to get an awful teacher for fifth grade, and when we got to school in September, we found we had Fishface McGill. The world's worst teacher. Or the time last fall when Danielle fell and broke her leg, right after she read a bubble gum wrapper that warned of trouble. Of course, you didn't need a horoscope to tell you trouble was coming there. Anybody with half a brain could have guessed it since she was trying to ride her bike with no hands — no hands, and she's a super klutz, and her equally klutzy little brother Tyrone was trying to help her. Still . . .

Still, I couldn't resist asking, "So what's going to happen? And to who? You? Or me?"

And why was I bothering to ask? Yes, I cared a lot about my Save the Earth project. And I even worried some about snobby Michele, who is always looking for ways to torment me. But that wasn't the really worrisome part. There was something much bigger worrying me. And if the horoscope was right . . .

"Both of us," Danielle said. "You know we have the same star. But you, being on the cusp" — she shook her head — "I hate to tell you this, but you're in worse shape than me. You who have always been super lucky, your luck will fail!"

Danielle is my best friend, but sometimes she's dumb. Lucky? Me? Didn't she wonder why I never invited her to my house anymore?

"You're weird," I said. "Weird, weird, weird!"

I sat up, bent over the edge of the bed, and dropped Jelly and Peanut Butter back into their shoe box.

Peanut Butter dropped right in, but somehow, Jelly tumbled over the edge of the box and ended up on the outside. Before I could snatch her up, she had disappeared under the bed.

"Help me, Danielle!" I yelled. "Jelly's out! She's under the bed! Quick!"

I jumped off the bed and knelt down beside it, and Danielle jumped down on the other side.

I looked under and saw Jelly disappear into a maze of dirty clothes and books and empty soda cans.

"I'll chase her; *you* trap her!" she answered.

Danielle started rattling and shoving things on her side and making swooping motions with her hands.

I saw Jelly coming, and I made a little cup of my hands — and she ran right into them.

But before I could close my hands tight around her, she had squirted out again back under the bed.

"Your side!" I yelled.

"Okay!" Danielle said. "Okay. Almost . . . There! Little beast. I got her."

She did have Jelly in her hands, but I could see Jelly was wiggling and thrashing around.

"Hey! Stop that!" Danielle said. "Hold still. Hey!" And then she yelled, "Oh, no!"

And she dropped Jelly and threw both hands up in the air, shaking one hand as if it had bugs or something.

"Oh, no!" she cried. "Oh, help! Oh . . . *yuck!*"

"What?" I yelled. "Grab her! Quick!"

Jelly raced across the floor, heading for the open closet door.

I got there ahead of her and slammed the door shut.

She turned around fast, then headed back to the bed, leaving a little trail of something behind her.

Was she peeing?

And Danielle — she had her hands over her face, and she was crying. "Dead!" she cried. "She's dead!"

"She's not *dead!*" I said, pointing. "There she goes! Help me!"

Jelly ran past again, and then suddenly she was gone. She'd been heading for the dresser, but when I looked under, she wasn't there.

I looked around. No Jelly. I didn't see her anywhere.

Danielle was crying — I mean really crying, sobbing practically.

"Will you hush up?" I said. "Help me find her."

Danielle took her hands off her face and pointed to the floor beside her.

"What?" I said.

She pointed again. Not speaking. Not sobbing anymore. Just pointing.

I looked.

7

A tail. There was a tail on the floor beside her. Definitely a tail. A gerbil tail.

We both stared at it. Then at each other.

Oh, no.

"I killed her!" Danielle whispered.

"You did not," I said, but my voice was all shaky.

And then I saw Jelly again, scooting across the floor between the dresser and the bed.

She definitely wasn't dead.

I raced for her, and this time I was faster than she was. I snatched her up and held her tight.

I turned her over gently and looked her all over. Except for not having a tail anymore, she looked pretty okay. She wasn't even too bloody, just a little rough, maybe — a little rough red place where her tail used to be.

"You okay?" I whispered to her, and I kissed her nose.

She snuffled at me some, just like always.

I set her back in her box and checked for Peanut Butter, who was already asleep in the straw there. I put the lid on the box, then put a shoe on top to hold it down.

"You can look now," I said to Danielle, who had her hands over her face again. "She's all right, I think."

Danielle uncovered her face and looked at the tail on the floor. "What about her tail?" she whispered. "Should we put it in the box with her?"

I shook my head. "I don't think so. I mean, it's off! Unless — maybe we should put it in the compost?"

"Her tail's *off?*" Tyrone said, poking his head in the door. "Wow! Cool!"

8

"Go away, Tyrone," Danielle said, pointing at the door. "Go!"

But he didn't. He came in.

"Is that its tail?" he said. And then, quick as anything, he picked it up. He held the end part up to his eyes, the part that used to be connected to Jelly.

"Tyrone!" I yelled.

But he was calmly squinting into it.

After a minute, he held it away. "It's empty inside," he announced.

"You are too gross!" Danielle said. "Get out!"

She jumped up and started shoving him toward the door.

He went and took the tail with him. Which was just fine with me.

"You think Jelly's going to die?" Danielle said after Tyrone was locked out.

"No," I said, although I wasn't at all sure of that. "But I think you better check on her lots tonight. If she looks sick, call me."

Not that I knew what I'd do if she was sick!

"I'm really sorry," Danielle said. "It was an accident."

"I know," I said. "It's not your fault."

"But you know what?" Danielle added, almost in a whisper.

"What?"

"The stars!" she said solemnly, her big brown eyes wide. "It's just beginning. The trouble, just like I told you!"

"It's not 'just beginning,' " I said, and I leaned in

close to her, so far forward our foreheads were bumping. "It was not the stars," I said firmly, "so stop being weird."

I backed up then so I could see her without crossing my eyes. "It was just an accident," I said.

She shrugged. But from the look on her face, I knew exactly what she was thinking.

"And nothing more bad is going to happen," I added. "Nothing!"

I put on my jacket because it was time to leave, time to go home to Jake.

"Nothing!" I said for the third time.

And I hoped, really hoped, that I was right.

Chapter 2

When I left that afternoon, I walked home from Danielle's the lucky way. It takes longer that way, but
Danielle had spooked me, even though I'd never
admit it to her in a million years. And with Jake, my
grandpa, being sick — well, I just felt as though I
needed luck that day.

To get home the long way, I walk all the way along
High Street, turn right at Lincoln, cross by the
park, and walk all the way around the park and then
home.

If I go the short way, I cut through the park and
come right out on my street directly. It takes about
fifteen minutes the long way, and about ten the short,
but that day it was worth it. It gave me a chance to
think, and it made me feel safe. Safe because if I could
bring us good luck, then I'd go home and find that
things were okay with Jake today.

Jake has only two kinds of days lately: bad and very
bad. On his bad days, he has trouble breathing like

always, but he can do most things. He works in our garden or in his woodworking shop and works on his quilt and cooks dinner — anything as long as it isn't strenuous, something that makes him use up a lot of breath.

But on his very bad days, he can hardly do anything but sleep. He doesn't even eat much. I guess eating and swallowing are hard when you can't breathe. For the past week, he hasn't even been able to get out of bed except to go to the bathroom.

He has some lung disease — emphysema, it's called — that he got from working in some factory when he was about ten years old — younger than me! He's always struggling for breath, and lately, since he's been in bed, he's been coughing a lot, too.

Sometimes, when he doesn't know I'm watching, I notice he looks very scared when he's struggling to breathe like that. But with Jake, I know not to ask. He doesn't even admit that there's anything really bad wrong with him. "So my lungs stink, so what?" is all he says about it. "People live with worse than this."

Me, if I have even a sneeze, he rushes me off to a doctor, but he won't go himself. When I tell him to see a doctor, he says, "What do they know?"

When I got home that day, I stopped at the mailbox by the street, checking for the letter the way I'd been doing every day since I was six years old.

But as usual, that letter didn't come for me. Just bills. A letter for me from the Wildlife Federation. And that ad that comes practically every week that says, Have you seen this child? with a dark, fuzzy picture of a kidnapped or missing child.

I always study those ads, thinking about what it would be like if I ever saw one of those kids and if I did, would I recognize him? I wonder if you could send out your own ads like that, only with a picture of a parent on them. Would anyone turn in missing parents? I wondered.

I never really missed my mom because she died when I was born. But Dad — my dad's been away a long time. Once, we all lived together, Dad and me, and Jake, too. But then Dad left to do something — he said he was going to join a group to save the whales and then he'd be back. I don't know if he ever saved the whales. He wrote for a while, and I still have his letters. I used to reread them at least once a week, but not so much lately. But then when I was about six, he stopped writing and hasn't written since. He hasn't come back either.

I started up the path to the back door, still looking at the mail. The Wildlife Federation wanted money from me. I didn't have any, but maybe I could make that part of my class project about saving the earth. Jake says I'm like my dad that way — always wanting to help someone or something or be involved in something big. I don't know about that since I don't remember my dad all that well. But while I'd never say it to anyone, I do wonder sometimes why my dad didn't want to help or be involved with Jake or me. But that doesn't mean I don't love him still, because I do. I just wonder.

13

Along the side of the house, Jake's garden still looked pretty good — cleared of weeds and ready for planting — pretty good considering that we hadn't worked there in weeks, since Jake's been sick in bed. Earlier this spring, we had turned over the soil and broken up the big clods of solid ground with a cultivator.

Every year after we plant, we have to find ways to keep out the rabbits and deer that come and eat up our garden. I wondered what we'd do this year.

Then, standing there, I saw something that at first startled me. And suddenly I began to laugh out loud.

I climbed over the fence and went to the back of the garden.

Foxes! Way back at the edge of our garden, there were foxes!

Jake had cut and painted wooden cutouts of foxes, propping them up with a stand at the back like I used to have for my paper dolls.

They were so lifelike that I almost expected them to move and jump at me. But then I thought, Wouldn't the rabbits and deer know they weren't real foxes if they didn't have a fox smell?

Weird. Jake is so weird! I stood there, shaking my head and laughing out loud. And then suddenly I had a thought, and I jumped back over the fence and went racing up the steps to the porch.

Jake must be better! He'd been working out here. He'd been in his wood shop, working!

I ran to the side door and up on the porch.

Yes! The quilt he'd been making was on the rocking

chair on the porch — so he'd been working on that, too. He was up; he was better!

I pulled open the kitchen door. "I'm home!" I called.

"No need to shout!" Jake answered, so close to me I was practically yelling in his ear.

He was standing right there in the kitchen by the stove, shaking a frying pan with some onions in it.

"Jake!" I said. "You're up. You're making dinner!"

"Brilliant!" he growled.

I ignored that.

"How do you feel?" I asked.

"How do I look like I feel?" he asked, turning to me and sort of thrusting out his chest. "Been working in the garden and wood shop all day. Got some supper going. Fit as a fiddle."

I looked him over.

He didn't look exactly fit, but he did look his usual weird self. Jake is really little, no bigger than me, and while I'm the right size for eleven, that's real little for a grown-up. He's not dirty or anything, but he does always look kind of — well, *different* would be a nice word for him. You could also say weird.

Like now — he was wearing baggy pants and his favorite navy hooded sweatshirt with double pockets in the front, all frayed along the edges. Years ago, he had used waterproof markers to black out some letters on the sweatshirt where it says — or where it used to say — EAST CAROLINA UNIVERSITY. Now, if you read it across, leaving out the missing letters, it reads: EST CARL VERSY. Jake says he likes it that way, that it sounds like the name of a lawyer. Why he wants to sound like

15

a lawyer, I don't know, unless it's because he never finished school and it makes him feel important.

He was also wearing his red high-top sneakers. Really. High-top sneakers on a grandfather. I keep trying to get him to get rid of them, but he won't. He was wearing loose white socks, drooping and sliding down into the backs of his sneakers. And his ankles were all swollen up as usual. Even with his high-tops half covering his ankles, I could still see that.

But he was out of bed! Making supper. And he was giving me that look that he does so often — half smile, half frown — as if he's making up his mind whether to laugh or to yell, both of which he does plenty.

I was so happy, I wanted to hug him — except that Jake isn't the hugging type and never has been. So I didn't hug. But I couldn't resist going over and kissing his cheek.

"Get along!" he said, and he turned away from me.

But I could see that he was smiling.

He nodded his head toward a jar on the table. "Open that," he said. I picked it up. Pickled onions. I hate pickled onions. But it didn't matter. I'd eat the jar! Jake was up, making supper. Looking just like always.

I opened the jar and handed it back to him, glad to see it was a glass jar, not a plastic one. When I turned, that's when I noticed the cigarette burning in an ashtray by the sink.

"You're smoking again!" I said.

"Yes, I'm smoking, and don't go scolding me. I'm an old man."

16

"An old man with rotten lungs!" I said.

"Mind your business," he said. "I'm allowed to have some vices. Set the table, why don't you? Do something useful instead of yelling at me."

I went to set the table, but it had been so long since we'd eaten in the kitchen, since we'd eaten anywhere but on a tray in his bedroom, that I had to clear the table of all the mail and newspapers — and of Roxy, who was curled up right in the center of the table on top of the paper pile. She is such a pretty cat — soft, reddish fur with white paws and a white bib. She's an old cat, but new to the neighbors. They just got her from the pound. For some reason, she seems to think this is her home.

I cuddled her close, bending my head to hear her little heart pumping away, to hear the purring inside her like a little motor.

I patted her for a moment, then put her gently on the floor. Then while I cleared things off and put the day's mail by Jake's place, I asked, "What'd you make for dinner besides onions?"

"Fried potatoes," he answered. "Put some onions in them. Bacon, too. Spinach with onions. And hamburgers —"

"— with onions," I added before he could finish.

"You got it," he answered.

He shook the frying pan. "I thought it was about time someone cooked a decent meal for you for a change," he said without looking up.

I shrugged. "I don't mind cooking," I said.

17

He laughed. "Wouldn't matter if you did, would it? Besides, you're a lousy cook."

"I am not!" I said, glaring at him. "You're just saying that because I don't put onions in everything like you do. Why don't you put onions on your cornflakes in the mornings?"

"It's an idea," Jake said thoughtfully, as if he was really considering it. "Beats strawberries or bananas, anyway."

"Maybe if you ate a piece of fruit just once in your life, you'd feel better," I said.

Jake made a face and hiked up his pants in the back. "Poison," he muttered.

I think he was only half joking. I don't think I've seen Jake eat a piece of fruit in my whole life. He buys fruit for me sometimes, but he never touches any himself.

When I had the table set and Jake had the meal ready, we took the food to the table and sat down.

When we were both seated, Jake bowed his head, and I did, too. Then Jake reached out and took my hand, the way he does every night.

We sat there quietly for a moment, holding hands, heads bowed, saying a silent prayer.

I wondered what Jake prayed for.

For me that night, with Jake's hand feeling so cold, I knew exactly what I was praying for, and I prayed even harder than usual.

After a moment of quiet, we let go of each other's hands and Jake picked up his fork.

"Now," he said, "tell me about the world of Brady

Abbott." Just like he had said for as many nights as I could remember.

And just like I had every night for as long as I could remember, I talked. Anything that was important to me was important to Jake. I have some friends who can't even talk to their parents, but Jake, I can tell him everything. Well, all but one thing that I never tell him — that I still think about my dad a lot. It seems unfair, disloyal or something, to hope for my dad to come back. I mean, Jake tries to be a dad. So I never mention that. Sometimes I dream about it, though, about how nice it would be to have a real family — a dad — like other kids have. Sometimes I imagine my dad would be just like Mr. Godwin, Danielle's dad. Mr. Godwin reminds me a lot of Bill Cosby.

That's the kind of dad I'd like, someone who laughed and played with me and who . . . I don't know, maybe was younger or something. A regular dad. Not at all like Jake, although I do love Jake a lot. I'm even named after him, although Brady is his last name and it's my first.

That night, I started by telling Jake the latest dumb thing Michele had said that day. She'd said that I look just like Ramona, only without the bangs. I hadn't known what she meant by that, so at lunchtime I snuck down to the library and got a Beverly Cleary book about Ramona and looked at the pictures. I still didn't understand, though, because I thought Ramona was a kind of cute little kid. And I sure knew Michele wouldn't intentionally be giving me a compliment.

"Do you think that's what she meant?" I said to Jake.

19

"That I look like a little kid? But I don't care about makeup and eyeshadow like Michele does. Besides, she needs that stuff. Otherwise she looks just like a ferret."

Jake cocked his head, frowning at me as though he was really thinking, assessing me. "You look fine to me," he said. "Just like your mom at your age. There'll be plenty of time to prissy up when you're older."

"That's what I think," I said.

Next I told Jake about my Save the Earth committee — the best part of school these days. Two weeks ago, Mr. McGill had given us an assignment for Social Studies — to come up with one important project that would help mankind, something that we could actually *do*. I've always cared about ecology and saving the earth, so for me, this was great. And I could get other people involved, too.

Next I told about going to Danielle's house and about Jelly losing her tail. When I told Jake what Danielle had said about today's horoscope, he just laughed. "She still believes that stuff?" he said. "I would have thought by now she'd have outgrown that."

"You don't believe it, do you?" I asked.

Jake looked up at me. "What're you, nuts?" he said.

"But Jelly's tail came off," I said.

Jake speared a fried onion. "For a smart girl, you sure say dumb things sometimes," he muttered.

"Still," I said.

"Still, trouble comes!" Jake said. "And no need to look to stars for it."

"Well, I know that!" I said. Then because I felt kind

of stupid, I added, "But you have to admit it was spooky."

But Jake just looked at me.

After he'd finished his second helping of fried onions, he put down his fork and lit another cigarette — another cigarette after he had bent practically double in another coughing fit.

"Jake!" I said.

He held up one hand. "Hush!" he said as soon as he could breathe again. "I didn't smoke a single one the whole time I was in bed, so don't have a conniption fit if I have one now."

"One?" I said. "You've had about six since I got home."

He grinned. "So you've been counting already?" he said.

"Yes, I've been counting. And it's dumb. It's bad for everybody — you, me, and the earth, too."

"Yeah, yeah, I know all about it. You know I don't usually smoke when you're around. But I'm not going to live forever, anyway."

"Yeah," I said. "But you don't have to speed it up, either, do you?"

Jake blew smoke up at the ceiling, then tilted back in his chair. "We should talk about that," he said.

"You're going to stop?" I said. "You going to try?"

"No. I mean that I'm not going to live forever. We ought to talk about that, make plans."

I just stared at him. "Plans?" I said. "What do you mean, 'plans'?"

"Plans, plans! Don't sound so surprised. Old people

21

die. Who's going to take care of you after I'm gone? We've got to think about that. It's been years since we talked to your dad. And who else is there?"

"You're not *old!*" I said.

"Seventy-eight," he said. "Old to be raising a youngster. I was a lot younger when I raised your mom."

"Seventy-eight's not old. Not today it isn't."

"Old enough. And I get these spells. You know they're not good."

His voice trailed off, and I could see him watching me.

It was the first time he had ever mentioned this. Ever said he was sick. Ever!

He must not be, I said to myself. He just has a cold.

I could feel something in my throat and chest, something knotted there, as if I had swallowed a lump of bread without chewing it.

I got up and started to clear the table.

He wasn't going to die. Wasn't. Wasn't!

I ran hot water into the dishpan in the sink.

"And when my time's up," he said, "you're going to need someone. Maybe it's time for some contact with a social agency. They might not be too bad. Or we could try again to find your dad."

I started singing. "Morning has broken," I sang, "like the first morning. Blackbird has . . ."

"All right, all right," Jake said behind me. "No need to get all worked up about it. I'm not dying yet."

"I'm not worked up! I'm *singing!*" I said. "And you're not dying, period!"

"Things die; people die," Jake said softly. "That's the way of it."

I whirled around, and soap suds flew from my hands. "Will you *stop* that?" I said.

He held up his hand. "Okay, okay," he said, and he wiped soap suds off the table. "I'm stopped."

But it was too late. Too late because it had been said. And all I could think was what Jake had just said at supper: Trouble comes. No need to look to the stars for it.

Chapter 3

Next morning when I woke up, I lay in bed for a long time, thinking. I was awfully worried about Jake. But some small part of me couldn't help feeling excited, too — excited because Jake had suggested looking for my dad. And we might find him if we looked. I would have a real dad, like Danielle has. If he would just come home, it would all be all right.

If Dad came home, he could help take care of Jake. Dad was grown up. He'd know what to do, how to get Jake the help he needed. This was the first time ever Jake had offered to look for him, had even mentioned my dad in years. So now I didn't need to feel guilty or disloyal wanting him back. Jake and I could try and find him together. And with Dad there, Jake would get better. I had even taken out Dad's letters and reread them the night before. I kept them hidden underneath one of Dad's old flannel shirts in my dresser. I used to bury my face in that shirt — it smelled like Dad. Dad had printed the letters because

I was too little to read script then, so they were kind of short. But in each one of them, he had said the same thing: "I hope Jake is taking good care of my girl." My girl. His girl. Me.

But how were we going to find him now? It had been a long time since he'd left, and sometimes I thought he was hiding. Still, with Jake helping, we'd find him soon.

What else to do for Jake? Get him to go to a doctor? Maybe get a housekeeper, a nurse?

But Jake would never let me do that, never. Besides, even though Jake is always saving for what he calls a rainy day, I had a feeling we didn't have money for nurses.

Where to begin? I didn't know, but all I could think was: Dad. My dad. Like a song, it kept going through my head. Jake and a real dad, too. I would find him — Jake and I would, together.

But when I went to school that morning, something happened that put Jake and even Dad out of my mind for a while.

As soon as we were all in our seats, Mr. McGill held out one hand, in that way he has that makes him look like a traffic cop or a school crossing guard. "Boys and girls," he said, "if you'll get settled quickly, we'll be hearing from each group about our Social Studies project this morning."

"Oh, good!" Michele said, looking down at her notes, as if she was talking to herself but loud enough for everyone around her to hear. "I have such a good plan — to include everybody! Wait till they hear."

Michele's desk is next to mine on the right, and Danielle's is on my left. We're all in the front, right in front of Mr. McGill. I saw Michele look up at Mr. McGill then and raise her hand, smiling and blinking fast.

For a minute, Mr. McGill didn't notice her, but that didn't stop her. She kept her hand up and kept right on with the eye stuff — blink, blink, blink, like a stoplight. It was a miracle she didn't get dizzy and fall facedown on her desk doing that. I don't know why she calls attention to her eyes like that. She has little squinched-up ferret eyes.

Finally Fishface looked up. "Yes, Michele?" he said.

"Mr. McGill?" she said. Blink, blink. "Could my team go last?"

"You're not unprepared, I hope?" he said.

"Of course not!" she said. Blink. "But I still want to go last." Blink and giggle.

Mr. McGill raised his eyebrows, but he just shrugged and smiled at her. "Someone has to be last. So yes, I guess it's all right."

"Oh, thank you," Michele sighed. She leaned across the aisle close to me then and whispered, "I like to leave the best for last."

I pretended I hadn't heard. *Best?*

I can't stand Michele. Jake says it's just that she's jealous, but I don't know. I do know that ever since first grade, when Jake was at school a lot, helping to design and build the school playground, Michele's been making fun of both Jake and me. Also, she's sneaky. She does mean things, but she pretends to act

26

so sweet at the same time. Like yesterday, her smiling and telling me I look like Ramona. Or the time last week when Jake brought my lunch to school when I forgot it, and he was wearing his high-top sneakers and his ragged old sweatshirt, and Michele acted as if she thought he was a homeless person who had found my lunch on the street. She leaned across the cafeteria table and whispered not to eat it, that she'd heard that homeless people spit in their food.

I wanted to spit in her food. Instead, I just told her to shut up, that he was my grandpa. Then she acted all embarrassed, as if she hadn't known, but I know she had. Jake's always at school, at the concerts and plays and parent conferences. It was one thing I didn't tell Jake about when we sat down to dinner that night.

Michele also competes with me for everything. Bruce Cato and I are the smartest two in the class — well, Bruce is *really* the smartest. But Michele acts as if I deliberately try to be smarter than her and as if she's in competition with me. Also, if I win something, like last year when I got to be editor of the class paper and she didn't, she does everything she can to ruin it. She said that a poem I had written was obscene and we shouldn't print it in the paper. I said she should mind her own business and that my paper didn't allow censorship. So then she told her mom, who came up to school and made a big stink about it. Michele and her mom won, and they made me change it. The bad word was *butt!* As if Michele had never said it in her life.

Anyway, that morning, Mr. McGill stood there waiting for everyone to get settled and get their notes out. When things were quiet, he said, "All right, boys and girls, let me remind you of the rules. There are twenty-four people in this class, six per committee. I assume each committee has met and done exhaustive work on this project. Today each group will tell us about the project you've decided on. You will outline your goals. You will list at least five *specific* ways that you might achieve those goals. And you will outline ways that the rest of the class will become involved for the next several weeks. This project is to be completed at the end of this marking period — six weeks from today. As you know, each committee will pursue its own project, and in addition, the class will decide by a vote which of the four projects we will take on as a *school* event."

Everybody already knew the rules, and really nobody but Michele seemed to be listening to Fishface. She was looking up at him as if she was hanging on every word. She had stopped the blinking, though. Maybe it had made her feel seasick.

"Ready?" Fishface said. "If you have your notes in order, you may now get together with your committees and choose a spokesperson."

Right away there was madness as everyone got up and began pushing desks and chairs around.

Fishface backed up to the blackboard, trying not to get trampled.

Danielle grabbed my hand, and together, we pushed our desks over to where the twins, Leslie and Lisa, were. We made a circle, and then the two Jasons joined us because they're also on our committee — not be-cause we wanted them but because Fishface said we had to have boys *and* girls on each team.

Jason Marks isn't bad, but the other Jason, Jason Cavanaugh, is a jerk. He's always making comments about girls' chests. Of course, he doesn't say much about mine because I don't have much of one, but last week, he even made a remark about that, too.

It wasn't hard to pick a spokesperson for my group: me. I had thought of the project and done all the work practically.

When all the groups had settled on their spokes-people, Fishface said, "Remember that this presen-tation also counts as part of your public speaking grade, so speak up clearly and remember the rules. Now, who wants to go first?"

Right away, Bruce's hand shot up. I think Bruce's hand automatically goes up when he hears a ques-tion. I bet if he dreams a question, his hand goes up in his sleep. Actually, though, his group idea was pretty good — they were going to work to help stamp out illiteracy. I wished I had thought of it, because one of the things they were going to do was work with kindergarten kids and write books with them.

I looked at Danielle. "Wish we had thought of that," I whispered. "Get us out of class."

"What'd Michele say before?" Danielle whispered back.

"She wanted to 'leave the best to last'!" I said. "Would you believe?"

Danielle drew a fast little sketch of a star on the cover of her notebook and pointed at it.

"Dummy!" I said.

Fishface frowned at us, and we both shut up.

Scott's group went next. They wanted to help the homeless. They had plans for bringing in old clothes and cooking meals and stuff. Not hard to do, and probably good, but boring.

I noticed, though, that when Scott first mentioned the word *homeless*, Michele poked her friend Susan Reid — another jerk and Michele's shadow, practically — they both even dress alike — and the two of them looked over at me.

I made fish lips at them, the way I do at Mr. McGill behind his back.

When Scott was finished, it was my turn.

"Good luck!" Danielle whispered.

I stood up and went to the front of the room. Fishface gives us grades for how we make every presentation. We have to speak clearly. We can't say "uh." And we have to make eye contact. Eye contact is hard because everybody tries to make you laugh when you look at them — everybody but your friends.

So I concentrated on looking straight at Danielle or Lisa or Leslie or my other friend Margaret while I talked. I told about our project. I told how we planned to achieve our goals. We'd recycle stuff in the cafeteria, we'd have a scrap-paper box in class so we could use the backs of papers, and we'd make a compost of cafeteria waste. And I ended with the best, one we were going to do right in the classroom: we were going to make a worm box on the windowsill and grow worms.

"*Grow* worms?" Michele said, right out loud, not even bothering to raise her hand. "How do you do that?"

"In dirt!" I said.

Michele looked up at the ceiling. "Brady," she said quietly, in this fake, super-patient way. "I have to tell you something. You need a biology lesson. Worms don't grow from *seeds!*"

A bunch of people laughed.

Fishface didn't laugh, but he said, "Brady, can you explain that — *growing* worms?"

It wasn't mean the way he said it, but from his voice, I had a feeling he was trying not to laugh, too.

I looked at him quick, but he seemed normal. He was looking down at his grade book, though.

"Just . . . grow them!" I said. "You put a pound of worms in a box. Then you add half a pound of scrap food. After a few weeks you've grown lots of worms and —"

"You don't mean *grow*," Bruce interrupted. "You mean *breed*."

"Well, they multiply, sort of," I said.

"Multiply?" Scott said. "In public?" And he began to laugh.

"Sexy worms!" Jason C. said.

Michele spread her hands. "But why would she want to do such a weird thing?" she asked — as if I wasn't even there.

31

"Because we need rich soil for the earth!" Danielle said loudly, sticking up for me and our project. "Worms make rich soil!"

"And baby worms!" Jason C. said.

The rest of the boys in the class got hysterical, and I could feel my face get hot. Even the other Jason was laughing.

Boys are so weird.

I didn't even try to finish. I just took my papers to my desk and sat down with everyone still laughing like crazy.

After a minute, Fishface said, "All right, boys and girls, that's enough."

He sounded as though he was choking, though, and when he finally looked up, I could see that his face was very red. I was sure he had been laughing, too, even though he had had his face buried.

He turned to me. "Brady, you and your group did a fine job. More than a fine job. I'm very pleased."

I didn't answer him.

"And we'll talk more about the worm box later, all right? Now, who's next?"

Danielle leaned close to me. "You did great!" she whispered. "You didn't say 'uh' even once. Just ignore Michele. And Jason C.! They're weird."

Michele stood up. "I'm next!" she said, and she stepped around her desk and stood there in the front.

Somebody whispered something about worm babies, and people started giggling again.

It didn't seem to bother Michele, though. She

just stood there waiting until everyone got quiet. It wasn't until they had all settled down that she began to talk.

I wished I knew how to do that. She could be a teacher.

"My project," Michele said. "I mean *our* project . . . is small. And simple."

Then she looked directly at me and smiled.

She's the only person I know whose smile doesn't make her look better. When she smiles, she looks even more like a ferret.

"Brady," she said. "Yours is important, I'm sure. It's just so . . . well, I mean, the *whole* earth? Ours is more personal." She turned to look at Mr. McGill then. "Our project is the family. We're working on bringing families closer together, all of our families here in this room and in the school. Because my father says the family is the basis of our society. Our committee has a list of things to do to help each of you bring your families closer."

She waved a big batch of papers that looked like Xeroxes of something.

"I'm going to hand these out in a minute," she said. "This is how to put together a family tree. My father says family history is important, too. Knowing our roots helps bring us closer together, he says."

She put down the lists and began unrolling a chart.

Susan Reid came up and helped her hold it up.

It was huge, sort of like a graph.

"See? Each of you has your name here," Michele

said, pointing her bright red fingernail to the names along the left side of the page.

Susan swept her hand down the page, like she was going, Ta-da! Pretending she was Vanna White on that game show, probably.

"You're supposed to find your name," Michele went on. "And each day, next to your name, you write down one good thing you did together with your family in the past twenty-four hours. It's an honor system, so everyone has to tell the truth. You can do things like reading to each other. You can play games with your little brothers or sisters or help with their homework. You could help your dad with his computer projects like I help my father. Or you could set the table or pick up the house for your mom when she's tired."

She sounded just like Mr. Rogers.

Danielle put two fingers in front of her open mouth, making a barf face.

Right. But at least Danielle could put stuff on the chart. She had lots of little sisters and brothers to read to, to play with, to pick up after. It's one reason I love being at her house.

At my house, Jake and I didn't read to each other. We never played games, except when I was sick and he played war or something with me. And I didn't have any little ones to read to. Or any mom to pick up for.

"But here's the best part!" Michele said, looking straight at Mr. McGill and doing her blinking routine again. "When the project is over, six weeks from today, could we have a Parents' Night, Mr. McGill? We'll share what worked best and how we've become closer. Our brothers and sisters can come, and our moms and dads . . ."

She stopped suddenly, as if she was thinking. Then she added, "People could bring grandparents, too. If they have to."

"That jerk!" Danielle whispered.

"A fine idea, Michele!" Fishface said. "This could be our school project."

I couldn't help it. My hand shot up, just as fast as Bruce's usually does. "You said we'd vote on it, Mr. McGill!" I said. "That the class could pick the best project to get the school involved."

"Well, maybe yes, maybe no," Fishface said. "Go on, Michele."

Michele smiled at me.

"I thought we could plan it for the last night," she said. "We could have like a celebration. And the ones whose projects didn't get picked, they could still show their projects off that night, right? Even maybe a" — she swallowed, as if she was deliberately forcing back a smile — "worm box. And wouldn't it be fun to have our moms and dads and brothers and sisters come to share with us?"

"It would, Michele," Fishface said. "I think everyone could profit from that. Whole families could learn from this."

I looked over at Jason C. His parents were divorced, and his mom and his dad had both gotten married again. I wondered if they all would come. He had too many parents.

But what if your whole family was just Jake? What if you didn't have any brothers or sisters? What if you didn't have a mom? What if you didn't know where your dad was?

Then suddenly, looking at Michele standing there looking so happy, so satisfied — so smug! — I made a decision: I would have a dad by the time that night came around. By Parents' Night, I would have found my dad.

Chapter 4

On the way home from school that day, Danielle tucked her arm through mine. "We'll share my family for this family project," she said. "My mom and dad already think you're one of their kids. There's so many of us, they'll never even notice an extra. You can come over anytime and stay over or eat over or anything. We can read to the babies and play with them or help Mom or whatever. Sugar always needs her diapers changed! And on Parents' Night, we'll all go to school together — Jake, too. Okay?"

I sort of hugged her arm.

"Thanks," I said. "But I think it's supposed to be real family."

"We're real family," she said. "Real family doesn't have to be just borned family. Right?"

I just shrugged.

Danielle is the best friend. The best. I was suddenly tempted to tell her about my dad, even though I had decided last night not to.

Danielle and I used to talk about him, how he disappeared and all. When we were little, we even used to play pretend games that we found him somewhere. We'd imagine that he was kidnapped, or held in prison somewhere. And I even remember once we spent a whole day in the woods, chopping off vines that were twined around a tree, pretending we were freeing him from chains. Of course, that was when we were just little kids. But now, thinking that he might actually come back was scary somehow. Too scary to talk about. Maybe because he might not be found. And maybe scary for other reasons, although I didn't know what they were.

So I didn't say it.

"We're just as much your family as if we were related," Danielle said. "In fact" — she grinned at me — "in fact, you can *have* Baby. That way she'll be your real sister."

I just laughed.

Baby is Danielle's little sister. Her real name is Carmen, but everybody calls her Baby, even though she isn't really the baby of the family anymore. There's a new baby, Sugar. Baby is my favorite of Danielle's sisters and brothers. She demands things and she yells, but she's so cute. And she can say practically anything, even though she's only two years old. The minute she sees me, she comes running to me. She yells, "Run, run, run — crash!" And she throws herself into my lap.

"Want to come home with me now?" Danielle

asked. "You could do some family stuff for the chart tomorrow."

I shook my head no. "Can't," I said. "I think Jake needs me."

"Is he okay?" she said. "You hardly talk about him anymore."

True. I didn't. But it was one of those scary things.

So all I said was, "He's kind of sick. Not too sick. But sort of. You know, he's old."

"Can we go play at your house?" she said.

"Can't really," I said. "Not today, okay?"

I just couldn't. Not until Jake got better. So I just said, "Got to go. I'll call you tonight, okay?"

She nodded and we said so long, and then I went the rest of the way home alone.

When I got in, I found Jake sitting on the living room floor, the middle desk drawer pulled out and resting on the floor beside him, and the entire contents of the desk spilled out around him — addresses, bills, letters. He'd been sorting out some of the stuff, and things were stacked up in separate piles. Roxy was asleep in the desk drawer.

Jake looked up at me when I came in. "I'm thinking about writing to the V.A. hospital," he said. "They should have records."

"V.A. hospital?" I repeated, puzzled. And then I realized. "You mean . . . my dad?" I said.

Jake nodded. "Your dad. An address, maybe."

He said it like it was a statement, but his eyebrows were raised.

I nodded and swallowed hard.

"What do you remember about him?" Jake asked.

I took a deep breath. What did I remember? Little things.

I put down my books, sat down on the floor, and reached over and lifted Roxy out of the drawer, pulling her into my lap.

"I remember," I said slowly, "that he used to be here with us. We'd dig in the dirt out front, make trails for my Matchbox cars under that maple tree on the days when he was feeling good. He'd bring me presents — licorice, the kind I like, the red kind in chewy sticks. Or pink balls, the high-bouncing kind. And on his . . . sad days, he wouldn't talk much. And I remember — I think I remember — when he first left, and there was just us, you and me. Later I used to write to him, afterward, at the hospital, and I'd put stickers on the letters, dinosaur stickers. Only, when he got out . . ."

I bent and stroked Roxy's rough, knobby head.

"When he got out," Jake finished for me, "he disappeared. Went to save the whales!"

"And never wrote me again," I said. I said it so softly, I could hardly hear myself.

But Jake heard.

"And you still look for letters from him," Jake said. "Still check the mailbox every single day."

"I do not!" I said. I looked up and glared at him.

But Jake was looking directly at me, a look so calm, so straight, that I had to look away.

I stroked Roxy's chewed-up ears, and they twitched.

"So what if I do?" I said. "I think about him some-times."

"Sure you do," Jake said softly, and his tone was so kind, so . . . something . . . that I had to quick bend over Roxy again.

"You been missing him?" Jake said.

I shrugged and I didn't answer.

"You're sure you want to find him?" Jake asked.

I looked up at him quick. "Why wouldn't I want to?" I asked.

This time, it was Jake who shrugged, and he didn't answer either.

"Of course I do," I said. "He could help us."

"Care for you, you mean?" Jake said.

"No! Not care for me. Nothing's going to happen to you, and you know it! I'd just like to . . . to see him again."

" 'Course," Jake said.

I would not tell Jake what I was thinking: that my dad would know what to do, how to help. He'd know because he was smart. He'd have to be to disappear so completely the way he had.

Smart, or sick, Jake said once.

Jake had taken me to the Vietnam Memorial in Washington one summer, the monument that lists the names of all the people who died in the war. Jake said there should be another monument — one where they list the names of people who got hurt bad, ones who came home and looked all right but whose brains weren't the same.

I knew he was talking about my dad when he said

that, but when I asked, he just shook his head and didn't say anything more.

So what was my dad like now, wherever he was?

That and other questions began haunting my mind, slipping in and out, questions I could not ask or even say to myself. Questions about why he hadn't come for me. . . .

But not now. I'd think about that later.

Jake was looking through the pile of papers; he picked something up and looked at me. "I asked you something before," he said. "If you've missed him. Do you?"

Did I?

"I . . . don't know," I said honestly. "I did. But it's been so long, I don't know how I feel now."

Jake nodded.

"Jake?" I said.

He kept looking at me.

"How come we never talk about him? Before this?"

Jake's eyes narrowed. "I don't know," he said, and he looked away.

But from the look on his face before he turned away, I figured he did know something, something he didn't want to tell me. Whatever it was, it made him mad.

But I didn't care what Jake thought or why he was mad. What mattered now was that we were figuring out how to get my dad back.

"I found this," Jake said, and he held out the paper to me.

I took it from him — not a paper, a picture. A photo of me when I was little — me and my dad, sitting side by side on the grass in front of the maple tree, me with a toy truck in my lap.

The tree was so small then!

And me, I looked so serious, staring out at the camera. My dad, he looked serious, too. Serious and so handsome, with thick, long hair, curling in front, and hanging over his forehead. And big, wide eyes.

I don't think I'm pretty, but I do have nice eyes — huge eyes, people say. They're a lot like my dad's, I could see now. Only my dad was handsome. I bet anything he was better-looking than Michele's dad.

He was holding my hand, too, holding it in his. Just the way I imagine sometimes.

"And you just a little tyke," Jake said, looking over my shoulder at the picture.

"So what about it?" I said. "Him leaving, you mean? He couldn't help it. You told me yourself he was sick."

"After that!" Jake said.

"So he had something to do," I said. "He wanted to save the whales." And then I had a terrible thought and I looked up from the picture. "He couldn't be . . . like . . . dead, could he?" I asked. "Like maybe he drowned or something?"

Jake shook his head. "No. We'd have heard. I'm also writing to where he was last, the address from his last letter. Don't worry. He'll turn up."

"Why didn't we — you — try before?"

Jake narrowed his eyes again. "Have tried. Some."

"But couldn't find him?" I asked.

Jake gave me a fierce look. "Well, he's not here, right?" he said, angrily. As if that was an answer.

But I guess it was. If Jake had found him, Dad would be here now.

I pulled Roxy closer to me and could feel her purring. "I need him by next month," I said. "Six weeks from today."

Suddenly Jake began to laugh. He laughed so hard that he began to cough, and then he laughed some more and coughed some more. He coughed so hard and struggled so for breath that I thought he'd faint. I watched him carefully, holding my own breath. Breathe! Breathe! I told him in my head.

Finally, finally, he did. He took a deep breath, then let it out in a series of small, shaky sighs.

"So what's so funny?" I said.

"You having me buried already?" he wheezed. "Give me just six weeks left, huh?"

"That's not funny!" I said. "You're not dying, and you know it. Just stop that."

I glared at him.

He laughed some more, then wiped his eyes.

"It's not because I think you're dying," I said, still giving him a dirty look. "That's not why I said that and you know it. It's because of Parents' Night. I want him here for Parents' Night."

Suddenly, Jake got very still. His eyebrows went up, and he seemed to be staring at me, studying me almost, as if he was seeing me for the first time.

"What's that look for?" I said.

He didn't answer.

"What?" I said again.

He still didn't answer, just bent and went to work on the papers again.

"I don't think that's very nice," I said. "Least you could do is answer me."

He picked up a paper and examined it. "I'm answering," he said. "So you want him here by Parents' Night, I got it. We'll just have to see if we can get him here then. For Parents' Night."

But there was something very odd about the way he emphasized the words *"him* here. For Parents' Night."

And I had no idea what was bugging him at all.

Chapter 5

Jake sent out a bunch of letters — to the V.A. hospital, to old addresses, anywhere we could think of where my dad might be. And then we waited. And waited. And waited.

Some letters came back, but no information, at least nothing that told where he was. It was as if he had just dropped off the earth.

Jake said I should stop worrying — that he was sure to be found and it was just a matter of time.

But time was running out. Parents' Night was coming — just four more weeks now. I didn't say anything more to Jake about Parents' Night, not since the way he had looked and sounded that day. I wasn't sure what had made him look like that, but the only thing I could think was too silly — that Jake was jealous. But that couldn't be, could it? Anyway, I didn't mention it again.

In school, our project to save the earth was pretty good, although we did have to abandon the worm box — and not because it was "weird" as Michele said. We had to abandon it because it stunk! Literally. I didn't mind the stink — I thought it smelled like rain, like the earth after a rain — but Fishface said it had to go. I think he said that because Michele made such a stink — I guess I mean a fuss — about it. So I brought the box home and put it in my bedroom. I kept it there for a week, and the following Saturday, I spread out newspapers on my bed and counted the worms.

Weird! I had even fewer worms than I had started out with. So how'd that happen? Were they hiding in the dirt? Or had they maybe eaten each other?

I called Danielle, and she said maybe they'd crept up and out of the box and had I looked on the floor and stuff.

That was a creepy thought, that they might be crawling around under the box or maybe even under my bed — or *in* my bed!

So I hung up, and then I dumped everything back in the box, worms and dirt and all, then shook out all my blankets. I looked carefully under the bed, too.

Nothing but dust balls under the bed, and Roxy down at the foot of my bed under the covers. I think I scared the wits out of her when I yanked the covers off her like that.

But there were no worms under the bed or in the bed. But maybe in another week I'd have more worms in the box.

At school, though, it was Michele's project that was getting all the attention, much more than ours. Mr.

47

McGill was even talking about calling the newspaper and getting them to cover the project. "Families and togetherness, a real newsworthy subject," he said.

Bet he was going for teacher of the year.

But worst was that each morning we had to record what we were doing at home on Michele's chart, what Michele called our "growth as a family."

Some people had neat things — reading to babies or playing games with little brothers or giving the little kids in the family their baths or baking cookies with their parents — all sorts of fancy stuff.

For Jake and me, it was all we could do to make supper and do the dishes every night. And even though Danielle "gave" me her little sister, Baby, and I actually did come and read to Baby some days, I wouldn't put it on the chart, because Michele would laugh at me. So instead, I started making things up. One morning I wrote that Jake and I had read *War and Peace* together. I had never read *War and Peace* in my life, but I knew it was one of the fattest books ever made. I read that in a book of lists somewhere. I also knew Michele was too dumb to know it would take a year to read it together.

Next day, I wrote down that Jake and I were planning a trip to some of the major religious shrines, to "increase our spirituality." I had actually read of a shrine somewhere in Austria that people were going to, but I didn't mention Austria specifically. Everyone would know that was a lie.

And then one morning, I wrote down that we were going to go without one meal a week to give that food to the homeless. Nice thought, but I'd never suggest that Jake go without food. He was too old. But I might actually skip lunch myself one day a week and give that food to the homeless shelter.

Michele always looked at my notes on the list and made some comment, but since she couldn't prove I hadn't done those things, all she could do was give me her superior smile.

I just smiled back.

Actually, I was getting pretty bored with all the projects. Six weeks was definitely too long to do this stuff, although Mr. McGill kept saying, "Imagine how long it would feel if you were truly homeless. Or hungry."

Yeah, yeah, yeah.

But it was still getting boring.

Then one morning, Danielle and Lisa and Leslie and I came into school and found something on the lunch menu posted in the hall, something that promised relief from boredom.

I looked at Danielle, and she looked back at me, grinning. "Do you see what I see?" she said. "Maybe the stars are changing. Opportunity time."

"Stars, nothing," I said. "Mashed potatoes!"

"Game time!" Lisa said, laughing.

"We're all buying, right?" Leslie said.

We all nodded, even me. Jake had made me lunch, but I had enough money to buy, I knew.

"But we still have to be careful," Danielle said. "This morning's horoscope said, 'Stay alert!' "

Leslie and Lisa just looked at me and shook their heads.

I rolled my eyes. All of us were sick of Danielle's horoscopes.

I couldn't wait till noon, and I knew the morning was going to drag. Finally, though, it was lunchtime and we all raced to the cafeteria to get our special table and start our game.

Leslie and Lisa are the ones who thought up the game. First you have to have the cafeteria table that's hidden by the pillar to play. Then you take a plastic spoon, load it with mashed potatoes, and when you're sure the lunch teacher isn't looking, you flick the potatoes off the spoon and up against the tumbling mats that are stored against the wall. Whoever gets the most hits that stick without breaking their spoon, that person is the winner. You lose as soon as your spoon breaks, and no fair getting another spoon. But the real loser is the one who gets caught and has to clean up the mats.

In just a few minutes of playing, I was ahead, three sticks to everyone else's two.

Danielle was already out with a broken spoon.

I had just loaded up my spoon again, ready and poised, when Danielle suddenly said, "Uh-oh. Trouble!"

I looked around.

"What?" I said. "Where?"

"Him. Fishface. Drop it."

She made a motion with her head over her shoulder.

I turned and looked.

Fishface. And Michele. In the back of the lunch-room. Both of them looking right at me.

I dropped my spoon.

Too late.

Fishface was heading in my direction.

"Stay alert!" Danielle whispered. "We didn't stay alert enough."

"I'm alert enough to murder Michele," I muttered back.

I looked at Michele, standing back there, her little pointed ferret face smiling at me.

But when she saw me looking at her, she mouthed something. From there, it seemed to be "Sorry."

Really?

In a minute, Fishface clamped his fishy hand on my shoulder. "All right," he said. "Up!"

"I'm going, I'm going!" I said.

I didn't even wait for him to tell me what to do. I had been caught before. It was no big deal. I got up, went to Mrs. Hazzard, the cafeteria lady, and asked for a sponge and some soap.

Mrs. Hazzard just nodded and gave them to me. She's used to this.

Fishface was standing at the table waiting for me when I came back. I started scrubbing the mats.

The recess bell rang then, and everyone jumped up, rushed to empty their trays and return them, then outside for recess.

"Want me to wait?" Danielle said to me.

"Don't bother!" Fishface answered for me. "Brady's chosen to forfeit her recess time."

I stared at him. *Who asked you?!* I thought. But of course I didn't say it out loud.

I just waved Danielle to go on. What did Fishface know? I had cleaned mats before. I'd have this done in no time at all.

I began scrubbing while he stood over me, watching.

"You missed a spot," he said after a while, pointing with his pale, pudgy finger to the edge of the mat.

There was a stiff gray blob on the mat there. I wiped at it, but it was like concrete.

"I didn't do that one," I said. "It's old."

"Who said you only had to wash off *new* dirt?" he asked.

"But I didn't do that!" I said.

He raised his shoulders and spread his hands.

Dope.

I went back to the spot. I rubbed and rubbed, but it wouldn't come off.

"I guess you'll have to try a different method," Fishface said.

I looked at the clock in the back of the cafeteria. Only twelve minutes of recess left. When I looked back there, I also saw Michele again. She was wearing rubber gloves and was going through the trash.

Weird!

I went back to Mrs. Hazzard. I borrowed a knife, a real one, not those plastic jobs like they give us kids, and brought it back.

I scraped at the concrete blob till it came off. There! In about two minutes, I had the mat clean — new potatoes and the old ones, too. Then I rinsed it off, and to show Fishface how wonderful I was, I even dried it with dish towels.

Perfect. Good as new, maybe better.

I returned the things to Mrs. Hazzard and wiped my hands on my jeans.

I looked at the clock.

Still three minutes left of recess.

"Can I go now?" I asked Fishface.

"*May* I go now?" he said.

"*May* I go now?" I said sweetly.

"No," he said.

"No?"

"No."

"Why not?"

"Why *not?*" he repeated.

What was this — ventriloquist time?

I just folded my arms and stared at him.

"I believe," he said, "that I just told you you'd forfeited your recess."

"But I finished the mat. It's clean!"

"And you won't have recess for the rest of this week or next week, either. You and Michele can work together."

"Michele?" I couldn't help being surprised. "You mean she's in trouble, too?"

"Of course not!" he said. "I mean . . . no. She's just very interested in ecology, though, in saving our planet and reducing waste. I believe she learned from you. And from Scott, too. Right now, she's documenting the food wasted in this cafeteria by weighing the dumped trash. You can help her. She's actually *doing* something to make a difference — while you and your friends, I'm afraid, simply talk about it."

Talk? Ha! I've been caring for the earth since long before our class project, since long before anyone in class even thought of it, Michele especially.

But I was too mad to answer. I just folded my arms and stared at him.

"That's why Michele brought your wastefulness to my attention," Mr. McGill said.

She did? She did!

I looked over at her, just as she looked up from her trash digging.

She smiled at me, her brilliant fakey smile.

I gave her a smile just as brilliant. And just as fakey. Because I was going to get her. I didn't know how. Yet. But I would.

Chapter 6

The rest of that week and the whole next week dragged — miserable, rotten time. No recess. And Michele was being a perfect jerk. I had to work with her *weighing* the *garbage* left over from lunch! And Fishface made me be the one to take the garbage out of the bins. All because she had told on me.

Also, Michele kept calling me Ramona, and then she'd clap her hand over her mouth and say, "Sorry. I mean *Brady*," as if she had really forgotten my name. Then one day, when I was bent over, head-down in a garbage pail, I heard her and Susan Reid come up behind me.

"Look at those skinny legs," Michele whispered — but I know she deliberately said it loud enough for me to hear.

"Doesn't she look like she's about eight years old?" Susan said, laughing quietly. "No shape. Toothpick legs."

I stood up and whirled around. "Well, at least I

don't try to look fifteen like you two do!" I yelled. "And besides, I don't have thunder thighs like some people I could mention!"

Actually, neither Susan nor Michele have thunder thighs, but I couldn't think what else to say.

They both just smiled and walked away, arm in arm.

That night I spent a long time looking at myself in the mirror.

Did I really look young, babyish — like Ramona without bangs?

I'd been noticing that some of the boys in class acted differently to certain girls. The boys showed off a lot, and they punched and poked certain girls, like my friends Leslie and Lisa especially. In fact, I wondered how come the twins weren't terminally black and blue.

But no boys ever punched me.

Not that I wanted them to. Still . . .

You could tell that the boys liked the girls they were punching.

And then I had a terrible thought: maybe my dad wouldn't like the way I looked, either. After being gone so long, wouldn't he want me to look grown up? He wouldn't want to come back and find that I still looked like I was six — or even eight, would he?

So what was an almost-twelve-year-old supposed to look like?

Danielle and the twins had been doing lots of makeup and stuff lately. But I hate makeup.

*   *   *

And then a week later something happened, something that was the final straw, that made me make a decision. I was at Danielle's house after school, holding Jelly up to my eyes, checking that her tail part was healing, and I happened to look in the mirror at that exact moment. That's when I noticed that my hair and Jelly's fur were the exact same color.

"Great!" I said. "I have gerbil-colored hair." I didn't add what else I was thinking, that if Danielle's mom was right — and a gerbil was just a fancy name for a rat — then I had *rat*-colored hair.

No wonder Michele had been making fun of me.

So I asked Danielle if she could fix my hair, and she came up with doing blond streaks. We'd have a makeover night, she said, a sleepover/makeover night while at the same time we planned some revenge for Michele. Because Michele had been doing really mean things, not just to me, but to everybody.

Danielle's mom said okay to the sleepover, and she even left money for us to order pizzas — twelve dollars for two large pizzas. She also let us have the house to ourselves a while, while she and Danielle's dad took her half dozen little sisters and brothers to the movies.

So now I was sitting by the sink in Danielle's kitchen, with Danielle and Margaret and the twins Leslie and Lisa standing over me.

"Okay!" Danielle said, waving a towel above my head. "You are about to be transmogrified!"

"Again!" Leslie said, grinning and showing her teeth like a mad doctor in a vampire movie.

"You know what you're doing *this* time?" I asked, watching Danielle pour some smelly stuff from one bottle into another.

"Of course I know!" Danielle said. "I've watched my mom do it a zillion times."

She looked up and smiled at me. When she did, some of the stuff in the first bottle dripped down the outside of the other bottle.

It looked *very* brown to me. Not at all like blond highlights, like we were supposed to be doing. We had already made highlights, but they had come out too yellow and we were redoing them, putting on some darker stuff.

"But your mom has black hair," I said.

Danielle shook her head. "Gray!" she said. "And not to worry. Besides, you said yourself, your hair is mouse colored!"

I just shrugged. Actually, I had said gerbil colored. Rat colored.

"Now hold still," Leslie said, taking the bottle from Danielle and beginning to section out my hair. "This is a despicable operation."

"Despicable?" I said.

"Yup," Leslie answered.

"You mean delicate?" I asked.

"No," she said. "And stop wiggling."

I held still. I knew she didn't mean *despicable*, but if it wasn't *delicate*, I wasn't sure what she *did* mean.

Leslie uses weird words, and it seems as though only Lisa, her twin, really understands her. I used to

58

think Leslie started talking weird when she was learning new words for the dictionary game that our third-grade teacher used to play with us. But then I realized that Leslie only moved here in third grade, so maybe she was using weird words even before that.

I held as still as I could for as long as I could stand it while Danielle and Leslie worked on my head. Margaret and Lisa went off to the family room, and I heard MTV come on loud. After a while, my head began itching, and my eyes did, too.

I was also worrying while they did it, and not just about my hair. I knew I was being stupid, that I was acting just like Michele, trying to get pretty. It's why I hadn't even mentioned to Jake what I was doing. It's not that he'd say I couldn't do it or anything. I was just afraid he might think I was as stupid as I thought I was. Especially if he knew it was for my dad.

In fact, come to think of it, maybe this *was* a despicable operation.

"My neck is killing me," I said to Danielle after a while. "Are you almost finished?"

"Yup," Leslie said. "A few more minutes and you'll be bald."

"Funny!" I said.

Danielle laughed quietly, and I thought she whispered something to Leslie, something that sounded a lot like, "Really."

Well.

"Is it supposed to look like that?" Danielle said then.

"Don't know," Leslie said. "Maybe."

59

"Like *what?*" I asked.

"Nothing. Hold on," Danielle said. "Let's try something else."

For a long time I could feel them rubbing my hair hard with a towel. They weren't pouring any color stuff on or anything — just rubbing it off. And they were awfully quiet.

"What's the matter?" I said after a while. "Is it awful? Is it ruined? Did something happen?"

"Nothing happened! Everything's fine!" Leslie said airily.

"Don't be such a worrier," Danielle said. "It's just that we have to leave the stuff on a while longer. It says right in the instructions that some hair is harder to take color than others. We didn't ruin you. It's just not changed.

"*Much,*" Leslie added.

I looked up quick, but she didn't look as if she meant anything special by that comment.

After a minute, Danielle took a plastic bag and put it on my head.

Great! Before, it was foil strips, now plastic bags.

"There!" she said. She tied it closed tightly with a plastic clip, then went over and set the timer on the stove. "Okay!" she said. "Rinse it off in twenty minutes. When the buzzer goes, wash it off, and you're done!"

I looked at my watch, making a mental note of when I would be done. *Done* made me sound like a loaf of bread.

But thinking about food, I suddenly realized I was starved.

I stood up, and the three of us pushed open the swinging door and went into the family room.

I looked at myself in the mirror over the fireplace.

I couldn't tell a lot because of the plastic — just goopy stuff piled on my hair. But I sure looked weird.

"I just hope there's not a fire," I said. "Imagine if I had to run out looking like this."

"Who knows?" Leslie said. "Maybe this looks better than the final product."

I picked up a sofa pillow to bash her.

"Just joking, just joking!" she yelled, ducking. "You're going to look great!"

Chapter 7

In the family room, MTV was on loud. Lisa was in front of the TV dancing to the music, and Margaret was on the floor doing leg raises to it, exercising her thighs.

Margaret is always exercising.

Always dieting.

And always fat.

I think fat's just in her genes.

I said that to her once, and she got very mad, because she thought I meant the other kind of jeans — like she had fat thighs in her jeans. But of course, I didn't mean that at all.

Danielle went over and picked up the phone to call pizza delivery, and everybody began yelling for the kind of pizza they wanted.

"Shush up, you guys!" she yelled back, covering the phone with one hand. "We have one with extra cheese and sausage. And one with what?"

"Hamburger!" Leslie yelled.

"One sausage, extra cheese, and one hamburger, extra cheese?" Danielle said.

All of us agreed, and she told the delivery person and then put the phone down.

"Guaranteed delivery in thirty minutes or less or it's free," Danielle said. She looked at me then and laughed. "We're going to make you answer the door."

I just made a face back.

I looked at my watch. I always hope they'll be late with the pizza order so we can get the pizzas free.

"I ordered low-calorie pizza once," Margaret said, hauling herself to a sitting position. She shuddered, and her curls bounced around her shoulders. She really has very pretty hair. "It was *so* gross!" she said. "It came with tuna and low-fat cheese. Like why bother?"

My thought exactly.

We all sat in a circle by the TV. Margaret came over to us, sort of walking over on her rump.

"Good exercise for the buns," she announced.

"So let's talk about Michele," I said. "How are we going to get even?"

"Did you hear what she said to me today?" Danielle said. "She actually lectured me about saving the earth — me! While she uses a new paper lunch bag every day, plus plastic bags for her sandwiches, and wastes tons of notebook paper."

"Yeah," Margaret answered. "And today she brought in Styrofoam egg cartons for her art project."

"And you know what she said about me?" I said. "She said she was going to have her dad ask Jake if we really had done all these things together."

"Boy, Jake will tell him off, I bet!" Danielle said. And then she added, "Is Jake any better?"

"He's okay," I said.

I felt bad that I hadn't been telling her the truth, either about Jake or about my dad. I didn't know why. Sometimes I wanted so much to tell her. But at the same time I was still too scared. What if we found him — and he said he didn't want to come back? Or what if he came back and he didn't like me? And about Jake — what if he was *really* sick? Somehow, talking about it made it too real. Also, talking about it when Danielle was promising trouble from the stars seemed to be asking for more trouble. Not that I believed a word of her stuff about the stars.

"Michele's father is such a jerk," Leslie said. She turned to her twin. "Remember, Lisa, last fall when Michele tried out for cheerleaders with us for Teeny League Football? And remember how she was wearing that skirt that was like about five inches long, and they made her go back and get gym shorts out of her locker like everybody had on?"

"Right!" Lisa said. "Only she couldn't get in her locker anymore because by then school was locked. And her dad took the whole thing of popcorn he had bought at the game and threw it at the judges, yelling that they didn't know anything about cheerleading and that they were all old football jocks. Michele got disqualified."

"They should have disqualified her father from fatherhood," Danielle said.

"Right!" I said.

"You should have seen how the judges looked though when that popcorn came flying in their faces!" Leslie said, laughing.

"How about something to make her look like a real jerk in front of her father?" Danielle said. "Like sabotage Parents' Night!"

"No!" I said quickly. "We can't do that."

Everyone looked at me.

I didn't want to sabotage Parents' Night. Not if I could find my dad in time. Not if I could bring him to Parents' Night.

But they were all looking at me funny, so I just said, "Well, I mean . . . you know, it just seems too mean. Not because of Michele. She deserves everything we do. But everyone else has worked hard at this. I was thinking of them."

"Yeah," Leslie said, "but so what? We should ruin it for Fishface, too. Well, not *ruin* it, ruin it. Just ruin it a little. He took this on as a school project without even a vote. And he had promised us a vote. I don't think that was at all fair. I mean, ecology and saving the planet are every bit as important as families."

"Right," Lisa chimed in. "There won't be any families if we don't have a planet for them to live on."

Leslie and Lisa smiled at each other.

I wondered what it was like to be an identical twin.

"We need a super plan," Danielle said. "Something that would really get even."

"Anybody have an idea?" Margaret said.

I did. At least, sort of an idea was forming. Something Lisa had said about sabotage. We could sabotage her locker. I had read about somebody using that packing stuff, those Styrofoam peanuts in a locker. But no, those things were environmentally unsafe. Still, maybe we could buy something else, some other packing that was safe.

"I have a plan," I said slowly. "It's maybe not super hideous, but it might work."

"What?" Leslie and Lisa said together.

I shook my head. I couldn't tell yet. I had to check something out first. But if we could buy it . . .

"We'll need money," I said.

"We could each contribute a little bit of our allowance," Danielle said. "Or ask our moms? But what's your plan? And where is that pizza guy?"

I looked at my watch.

Twenty minutes since we had ordered. I hoped the delivery person would get lost and would be late and we'd get free pizza.

And then I had a thought, a money-for-getting-Michele thought, a money-for-meanness thought! It was right here. Twelve dollars for two large pizzas, extra cheese! Plenty of money for what I needed.

I looked at my watch again, then at Danielle, then at the money on the table.

"If we get free pizza," I said, "can I keep this money to use for the get-Michele project?"

Danielle looked doubtful. "It's my mom's."

"I know," I said. "But what if the guy gets here late?

66

And what if he gets here late because of something we *do?* Because of my plan?"

Danielle shrugged. "I guess. But you can't *make* him get here late!"

"Want to bet?" I said. "Watch this."

I got up and went across the room to the big picture window.

It was already dark out, and we had all the lights on, including the porch light.

I switched off the porch light.

Then I closed the drapery across the window.

Then I turned out all the lights in the family room and switched off MTV.

"Hey!" Leslie yelled.

I could see that a light was on upstairs.

"Danielle, go upstairs and turn out the lights up there," I said.

"*O-kay!*" Danielle said, and I could tell from the way she said it that she had caught on. She jumped up and bounded up the stairs.

In a second, the place was completely dark.

"But how is this going to work?" Margaret said. Her voice sounded weird, coming through the dark.

"Because he's looking for a house that looks like people are waiting for him, a house with lights on," I said. "With the lights out, this'll look like nobody's home. It'll be harder to find, hard to see, and it'll confuse him. That means it'll take extra time. His time is almost up now."

In a minute, Danielle was back downstairs.

It was so dark it was almost impossible to see, but

there was a tiny gleam of street light coming in through the window that faced the driveway — just enough to see my watch. Just enough to see that it was twenty-six minutes since we'd ordered.

"How much time?" Leslie whispered.

"Four more minutes," I said.

A car came down the street, followed by another car.

But they went on, neither car stopping.

"Three more minutes," Lisa whispered.

"Twelve dollars!" Danielle answered.

Another minute passed. Another car came down the street.

We sat absolutely still and silent, practically all of us holding our breath.

Then we heard it. Out on the street. A car stopped. A car door slammed.

Footsteps on the porch.

The doorbell rang.

And Leslie and Lisa said identical bad words.

Chapter 8

My hair!

I'd forgotten my hair! We were eating pizza. And had forgotten my hair.

I was in the middle of my second slice of pizza when I looked at my watch.

Forty-five minutes!

"Oh, no!" I yelled, and I dropped the pizza.

I jumped to my feet and stepped right in the middle of the pizza box — the open box with pizza still in it.

It was hot!

"Pizza foot!" Lisa yelled.

"Toe cheese!" Leslie said.

"Get out of there!" Margaret yelled.

Only Danielle seemed to realize what was happening.

She jumped up with me. "Hurry!" she yelled.

I backed off the pizza and wiped my cheesy foot on the rug. I yanked at the plastic bag on my head.

"Help!" I yelled. "Help get this off!"

"Come on!" Danielle said.

We raced to the kitchen, with the others suddenly jumping up to follow.

When we pushed open the swinging door, we heard the buzzer going.

Why hadn't we left the door open?

"It's ruined!" I said. "I know it! Ruined."

"No, it's okay," Danielle said. "It's okay, I promise. Don't worry. Don't panic."

"Who's panicking?" I yelled.

"Just stick your head in the sink," Leslie said.

"Stick your *foot* in!" Lisa said, laughing.

"Hurry up!" Danielle said. "Under the faucet."

I raced for the sink, and Leslie quick turned on the water.

I stuck my head way down under the faucet.

"It'll be all right!" Danielle kept saying. "It'll be all right."

But I didn't believe her for a minute.

I stayed bent over the sink while both Leslie and Danielle worked on my hair, spraying it with the hose attachment and rubbing it hard.

Someone went and turned off the buzzer.

Suddenly it was very quiet in the kitchen.

"How is it?" I asked. "How's my hair? How's it look?"

"It's . . . okay," Danielle said.

"Let me see it!" I said, and I started to straighten up.

But Danielle leaned hard on my shoulders, pushing me back into the sink.

"It's not finished yet!" she said. "It's still rinsing out."

I could see the rinse water pouring off my head and down into the sink, and it was a goopy, ugly brown. Maybe gerbil color was better.

Leslie and Danielle were both working on it now, Danielle rinsing, Leslie rubbing it. They both began shampooing, and I could see shampoo suds floating down the drain then. But nobody was saying anything.

"It's ruined, isn't it?" I said.

"Not . . . ruined," Leslie said.

I started to try to get up again, and again Danielle pushed me back. She bumped my head on the faucet.

"Ouch!" I yelled.

"I'm sorry, but will you *wait?*" she said. "I'm still rinsing."

I stayed bent over. Around me I could see their feet — eight feet, all four of my friends gathered around the sink. And not one of them was speaking.

Horrified — that's what they were.

I backed out of the sink then, making sure my head was out from under the faucet, and stood up.

This time, nobody tried to keep me down.

Water was dripping off my hair, and I grabbed a towel.

Everybody was watching me.

Danielle looked a little scared.

Leslie and Lisa — I had a feeling they were both trying not to laugh.

And Margaret was leaning against the edge of the sink, still eating pizza and looking at me, her head tilted to one side. "It's not that bad," she said, her mouth full.

I went to the family room and over to the big mirror.

And stared at my hair.

At my totally green hair.

No, that's not true. It wasn't totally green. Most of it was regular gerbil or rat colored. It was the other parts, the streaks that were supposed to be blond — those were green. Really. Not grass green, but definitely a dull, moss green.

I rubbed my hair with the towel, then checked the color on the towel. No green came off.

Slowly, I went back to the kitchen.

Danielle had her back to me, mopping up the sink.

Leslie was reading the back of the hair color box — a little late for that!

Margaret was still eating pizza, and Lisa had joined her.

"Great!" I said. "And you all said you knew what you were doing."

"It's not my fault nobody heard the buzzer!" Danielle said.

"Maybe when it's dry it'll look better," Leslie said. She went over to her sister and leaned against her, reaching for a bite of Lisa's pizza. "Remember, Lisa," she said, "when we first decided to get our hair cut in layers? Remember how afterward, we both thought we looked just like artichokes? But after it got dried, it was fine. It lay down just right."

Right. Only mine wasn't cut like an artichoke. It

was the color of an artichoke. And drying it was not going to change it.

We were all standing around, looking kind of glum, when suddenly the kitchen door burst open and Danielle's little brothers came racing in, led by Tyrone.

I grabbed the towel and wrapped it tight around my head again.

"Why are the front lights out?" Tyrone yelled. "What a great movie, you shoulda come." And then he looked at me. "What'd you wash your hair for?"

"What do you think?" Danielle said.

I didn't say anything.

Then Mr. and Mrs. Godwin came in, Mr. Godwin carrying the littlest baby, Sugar, and Mrs. Godwin carrying Baby. Sugar was asleep on Mr. Godwin's shoulder, but Baby was wide awake and squirming to get down.

"Hi, girls!" Mr. Godwin said, speaking softly so as not to wake up Sugar. He smiled at us, his perfectly gorgeous smile. He really is awfully good-looking for a father. "Have fun?" he asked.

Nobody answered.

Mrs. Godwin said, "Uh-oh!"

"Down!" Baby demanded. "Put. Me. Down."

She said each word like it was a separate sentence.

"Nope!" Mrs. Godwin said, holding tightly to Baby. "You girls look like you need me."

"Really," Mr. Godwin said.

"We're okay," Danielle said.

Mrs. Godwin looked doubtful, and Mr. Godwin reached out to take Baby from her.

But Danielle said, "Mom! Dad! We're fine! Really."

Mr. and Mrs. Godwin just looked at us, then exchanged looks with each other.

Then Mrs. Godwin shrugged. "Come on, troops!" she said to the little ones. "Up you go. I think these girls want to be alone."

She and Mr. Godwin both started for the stairs, herding the little ones in front of them.

At the foot of the stairs, Tyrone stopped and turned to me.

"Brady?" he said. "I threw away the gerbil's tail, okay? It began to stink."

"Thanks for telling me that," I said.

Danielle giggled, but she shut up when I glared at her.

When the rest of the family had gone upstairs, I went back to the family room, unwrapped the towel, and looked at myself again in the mirror.

I looked absolutely gross. And I was absolutely furious.

But I realized, too, that it wasn't anyone else's fault but mine.

I had decided to color my hair. I had decided to be a jerk and try to change my looks like Michele wanted me to. I had decided to get fancy-looking for my dad. I had forgotten to check the time.

It was no one's fault but mine.

And now I had to decide what to do about it.

I peered in the mirror again. The streaks were very green.

There was only one thing to do. Cut them off. Cut off all the green parts. It would probably be pretty chopped-up looking, but at least it wouldn't be green and I wouldn't look like a freak.

Well, maybe I'd look like a freak, but at least I wouldn't be a green one.

I went back to the kitchen.

Everyone was just standing around silently, as if they were waiting for a bus.

I went over to the drawer by the sink, the one Danielle calls the junk drawer, and rummaged through it till I found the scissors.

Then I went to the table, sat in a chair, and held up the scissors. "Cut!" I said to Danielle. "Cut off all the green parts."

"*All* the green?" she said.

"All," I said.

"I'd have to cut it right at the scalp to get all of it!" she said.

"So? Cut."

She was staring at me.

Everybody was staring at me.

"It'll look awful!" Danielle said.

"Gross!" Lisa said.

"Really gross," Leslie said.

"Worse than now, you think?" Margaret said.

There was a long silence.

It was scary — really scary — that nobody answered that.

That did it!

"Cut!" I said again.

Danielle took the scissors from me and began cutting.

And all the while she was doing it, I could hear her muttering something. "Blame it on the stars."

Stars? Ha!

Blame me. Stupid, stupid me.

And wait till Jake got a load of this!

Chapter 9

"Okay, so I made a mistake!" I said to Jake. "I ruined my hair. Now leave me alone." I made a face at him. "Don't have a conniption fit," I added.

It was Saturday afternoon, the day after I had wrecked my hair, and I was sitting on the porch with Jake — sitting there with my half-chopped-off, half-green hair. Danielle had stopped halfway through cutting and made me look at it in the mirror. Boy, was it a mess! So we had decided not to cut any more. Now, instead of looking like a complete punk, I just looked like *half* a punk.

Geez.

"Who would have believed?" Jake said softly, as if he was having this nice quiet conversation with himself. "Who would have believed I'd live long enough to see a person with green hair? Honest to God."

He made a clicking sound, his tongue against his teeth, then rocked back in his chair.

Roxy jumped on the porch railing, and I snagged

her and pulled her close, snuggling her to me. She settled into my lap, warm and soft.

For a long time Jake didn't say anything more, but he kept making that irritating clicking sound.

After a while, he sighed and said, "Green hair! For such a smart girl, you sure . . ."

". . . act dumb!" I finished for him.

Again we sat silently.

I cuddled Roxy in both hands. She didn't seem to mind if I had green hair. I listened to her heart going furiously fast. I wondered why cats' hearts beat faster than people's hearts. I wondered, too, if cats' hearts hurt or got sad, like people's did.

I was feeling sad that day, very sad. And it wasn't just my hair, although that was terrifying me — the thought of going to school on Monday. And facing Michele. But more than that, it was Jake.

Just watching him walk so slow, watching him struggle for breath, made me sad. And here it was, a pretty spring day, the nicest in a long time, and we weren't even working in the garden. Jake could hardly walk at all without having to stop every other step to catch his breath.

I should have been here with him last night, and not just because it would have saved my hair. Jake hadn't even gotten up till I got home that Saturday. He said it was because he was tired. But I had a feeling he was afraid to be up and around the house without me there.

"Want me to make you lunch?" I said after a while.

Jake shook his head. "No. Gotta talk," he said.

"Nothing to talk about!" I said. "I screwed up my hair. It'll grow back. Forget it."

"I didn't mean your hair," he said.

"What?"

"Your" — there was a long pause — "dad."

I sat straight up and stared at him. "What?"

Jake nodded. "Yeah, your dad."

"What about him?"

"I know his . . . whereabouts."

"Where?" I said. "Where is he?"

My heart was hammering so wildly it could have competed with Roxy's. "Is he all right?" I added.

"Far as I know he is," Jake said.

Then Jake leaned forward suddenly, both hands clutching his knees.

He began to cough. And cough.

I could see his hands and knuckles turn white, he was clutching his knees so hard.

When he stopped coughing, he straightened up. "I'm all right now," he said. But he was breathing heavily, and he looked anything but all right.

Suddenly he started to get up. "Maybe I do want lunch," he said.

"I'll do it!" I said.

But Jake was already heading into the house, so I just stood up, too.

Roxy was asleep in my lap by then, and I gently transferred her to the chair.

She didn't wake up.

"What do you know?" I asked as we went into the house. "Where is he?"

Jake didn't answer. Instead, once inside, he went directly to the sink and took a long drink of water.

Then we both set about getting some food, neither of us speaking.

Jake got out stuff from the refrigerator, and I set the table and made coffee.

I didn't know what Jake was thinking, what had happened, but my mind was going wildly. Dad. He had talked to my dad.

But no, I bet not. He would have said so right off. He just knew where he was. But then . . .

Jake brought some cold cuts and bread and onions and a small cutting board to the table and then sat down, leaning back heavily against the chair for a moment.

When he had caught his breath, he began slicing the onion carefully into thick, even slices.

"Are you sure you want to see him?" Jake asked, as if it was the most normal thing in the world to say.

"See him?" I said. "Of course!"

Jake nodded and went on slicing the onion neatly in smooth, even motions.

He could be a surgeon the way he carves.

"He lives no more'n an hour away," Jake said.

The slices of onion fell slowly to the cutting board, a small cascade, slice upon slice.

I sat down so abruptly, I almost knocked over a chair.

Jake looked up at me quickly, then away.

We had his address. An hour away! So close!

What if I called, what if I said, "It's me, Brady?" And he didn't know who I was? Or what if he knew, and wished I hadn't called? What if I could tell that?

The thoughts raced back and forth, like a war inside me.

And then I thought of my hair. My hair! I looked like a weirdo with my spikes of green hair! He'd think I was a punk rocker or something.

I put both hands to my head and groaned.

"What?" Jake said, looking up from his slicing again.

I took my hands away from my hair and shook my head. "Nothing," I said.

I got up and went to pour Jake's coffee.

I got his mug from where he keeps it on the windowsill, poured in the milk and coffee, then brought it to the table and sat down.

Jake was making himself an onion sandwich, thickly buttering two slices of rye bread, then layering on the slices of onion.

When he had it fixed to his satisfaction, he sprinkled it with salt and pepper, put the top slice of bread on, then neatly cut the sandwich in half and picked up one half.

But before he took a bite, he looked right at me.

"Cat got your tongue?" he said, but he said it kindly.

I just shrugged and shook my head again.

There were so many things I was thinking. Like what were we going to do next? Where had he been? When was he coming? Would he help care for Jake? Did he have money to help?

Did he want to see us?

Did he want to see . . . *me?*

And the thought I couldn't keep out, even though

81

I kept trying to shove it aside: if he lived just an hour away, why hadn't he come back for me before?

But with all the important things to ask, I ended up asking something dumb. "How did you find out where he is?" I asked.

Jake frowned at his sandwich. "Two places. The V.A. hospital had his address, but it was old, from years ago, they said. And it took them forever to even trust me that I had a right to know! As if his own daughter shouldn't know where he was! Anyway, next I called Information in the town the V.A. finally told me about and asked for a William Abbott at that address. Well, they only had one William Abbott — at a different address — so I called, and sure enough — it's him, your dad."

My father. All I had to do was pick up the phone.

"So how soon you think you'll want to see him?" Jake asked.

"Did you talk to him already?" I asked.

"Next week, maybe?" Jake said. "You think you're ready?"

"What do you mean next week?" I asked. "Did you already talk to him? Write to him? What? Will you answer me?" I glared at him.

"I . . . talked to him," Jake said.

"You did?" I said. "What'd he say?"

No! I jumped up from the table and went to the fridge for the ketchup. Thoughts were chasing each other round and round in my mind, like my gerbils chase each other on their little race thing. I didn't want to know what he said. What if he wasn't happy to hear from us?

But of course he'd want to hear from me. I was his daughter.

His girl.

I came back and sat down.

Jake took a big bite of his sandwich. He chewed for a long time, and then he put down his sandwich and said, "He wants to see you. Next week, if it's okay with you. But let's think about it awhile. Let's let it cook in our heads a few days before we decide what to do. No need to rush anything."

Next week. If it's okay with me. He's coming home.

I just sat there, running my hands over what was left of my hair.

Jake was looking at me carefully, his head tipped to one side, and I saw that funny look he gets sometimes — that about-to-laugh, about-to-yell look.

Suddenly he got up from the table. "Stay here!" he said. "Be right back."

He headed for his bedroom, shuffling a bit, his bedroom slippers making a soft *hush, hush* across the floor.

For some reason, I had a feeling he was going to get a photograph, a photo of my dad.

But when he came back, he wasn't carrying a photo at all. He was carrying a book — a phone book — the yellow pages.

He dropped it on the table in front of me. "Look up beauty shops!" he said. He sat down heavily in his chair. "Then go have them do something with that head of hair — or whatever it is you call it."

Then he reached over and stuck something in my hand — a bill, folded over and over till it was hardly bigger than a matchbook.

I unfolded the bill. I stared down at it, then up at him. And then I shoved the bill back at him.

"I can't take this!" I said.

It was a hundred-dollar bill, probably one he was saving for his "rainy day."

But when I pushed it back at him, he just held his hands up.

"Keep it," he said.

"I can't!" I said.

"You got to," he answered.

"This is your savings," I said.

"Right," Jake said, laughing. "With a head of hair like that, it's a good thing we got some savings."

And even though he was laughing, I had a feeling he was very serious.

"Go get yourself fixed up," Jake said quietly. "You don't want your dad to see you like that."

No, I did not want my dad to see me like that. But then I had a scarier thought: Was I really sure I wanted to see my dad at all?

Chapter 10

Each day is just twenty-four hours long, and each two days is just forty-eight hours long. I know that. But that weekend was as long as a month. And the whole next week felt like about a year.

Because my dad was coming. Saturday.

I took out all my dad's old letters and reread them. They seemed so babyish now, but I guess that's because I had just been a little kid when he left and wrote them to me. Each letter ended the same: "I hope Jake is taking good care of my girl."

His girl. Me.

On Monday, I went to school, just like every other day. But it felt so weird. How could I go to school when everything felt so different?

At school, first thing I had to do was face everyone about my hair.

The hairdresser had rescued it pretty much, but it was *awfully* short! She had to make it super short to match all the parts we had cut. But at least she had been able to cover what was left of the green so that it was about the same color as the rest of my hair: gerbil colored. And she said it would stay that color as long as I didn't "mess" with it again.

I sure could promise that. Even gerbil or rat color was better than green. Only thing was, it had cost seventy-five of Jake's dollars to get it gerbil colored again. And I just hated that. I'd have to find a way to pay him back.

When I first came in with Danielle that day, lots of people made comments. A couple of the boys laughed, and Jason Marks said my hair was shorter than his even, which was true, but he said he liked it that way.

"Funky," he said.

Bruce called it "outrageous," but I couldn't tell if he meant that as a compliment or not.

And then there was Michele. She was standing talking to Mr. McGill when I came in, and as soon as she saw me, she slapped a hand over her mouth and whispered, "Oh, *weeeeeird!*"

That's exactly how she said it.

Mr. McGill frowned at Michele, then smiled at me. "Why, I like it, Brady!" he said. "Very . . . New York."

I didn't know what that meant, but the way he said it, it sounded like a compliment. Which really surprised me. It surprised Michele, too. You could see that from the look on her face.

Somehow I made it through that day, forcing the thought of my dad out of my head. And then something happened that made me forget my dad completely for a moment — a great moment, when I knew just how we could get even with Michele.

It was late afternoon, and we were having that free period just before we go home when we're allowed to work on our projects or just do homework or whatever we want. It's always noisy and crazy, and even with Fishface, it's still a fun time.

As soon as the class was settled into our free time, Michele asked Mr. McGill if she and Susan could make an announcement. "About something special for Parents' Night!" she said.

He nodded, and Michele and Susan went and stood up front. Michele was blinking at everybody in that weird way she has, and Susan was practically buried behind a huge brown paper bag stuffed full of something.

"Boys and girls!" Michele said. "Could we please have your attention?"

" 'Boys and girls'?!" Danielle whispered. "Does she think she's the teacher?"

A whole bunch of people began laughing, while others continued to talk between themselves, bent over their projects.

It didn't bother Michele, though. She just stood there, waiting. Finally she said, "When you're all quiet, we'll go on."

A bunch of people laughed, and then Fishface chimed in. "Unless perhaps you'd like to stay after and then you can hear what Michele has to say."

That shut everybody up.

"Thank you," Michele said. "Now, we're going to serve refreshments for Parents' Night. We want brownies and cupcakes and even candies. But we want only home-baked goods, something you make together with your parents — even the candy. I'm passing around a list so we know what each person is bringing. And we'll be very careful to have no duplicates. We all know how important it is not to waste food."

She looked right at me when she said that. And then she added, still looking at me, "If you can't bake anything, you can donate money if you have to."

I smiled at her. I had made up my mind last week to get even. Let her wonder about the smile.

Susan put down her grocery bag and handed the list to the first person in the front row: Bruce.

Right away, he started writing. He wrote and wrote.

Was he having his mother supply enough food for the whole school?

"And on Parents' Night," Michele added, "we're going to have a sign-in book, so we know who came and who brought their parents. We can keep it forever. I have this guest book" — she held up one of those blank books you can buy — "a permanent reminder of our parents and of Parents' Night."

A permanent reminder. Of Parents' Night.

A permanent reminder of the first night I would ever have a *real* parent at a school night. Not just Jake. My dad.

"Now," Michele continued, "I have a little gift for all of you, from my mom and Susan's mom. We spent all weekend making these, as part of our family project."

Susan picked up the grocery bag that was on the floor in the front, and she and Michele started going up and down the aisles, handing out what was in the bag.

Popcorn balls. I hate popcorn balls.

When Michele handed Danielle hers, I saw that it was wrapped in plastic wrap, shaped like a bell, with a small note attached.

I leaned over and read it. The note said, "This little bell comes with love from Michele. And Susan."

Oh, barf.

When Michele handed me one, I put my hand out, pushing hers back. "No thanks," I said. "You wrapped them in plastic. That's environmentally unsound. You should know that."

"Besides, they're probably stale!" Leslie said.

"Are not stale!" Michele said.

"Bet," Leslie said. "They're probably from popcorn left over from those football games."

Michele's face got red, and she just huffed off.

"Bet they are, too," Lisa said. "I wonder what our dad's going to do with all the popcorn we have left?"

I turned to them. "You have popcorn left over?" I said.

"Sure," Leslie said. "I told you, from the football games. Our dad works the concessions, and there are bags of it left in the garage. We have to feed it to the birds or something."

I started to smile.

No we didn't. We didn't have to feed it to the birds at all. It was even better than what I had first thought of — those Styrofoam peanuts.

Popcorn is environmentally safe. But it is very, very messy if it's in the wrong place. Like a locker. But then *I* would have to use plastic wrap. Could I?

Leslie took her popcorn ball and began to poke at it with her pen. "Stick needles in her eyes," she said, poking a pen viciously into the plastic around the popcorn ball so that bits of popcorn came squirting out.

"It's against the law," Lisa said.

"I have a better idea," I said quietly. I grinned and leaned over close to Danielle and Leslie and Lisa. "Popcorn," I said. "Can we use the leftover popcorn?"

"It's no good, really," Leslie said.

"Oh, yes, it is!" I said. "We're not going to eat it. We're going to get Michele with it. And . . ." I hesitated. "Plastic wrap? Can we get some?"

"Plastic wrap? You?" Lisa answered. "Our mom has some. Lots of it. Even though I told her she should stop using it."

I put an arm around Leslie and one around Lisa, pulling them all in close so that all four of us had our heads close together.

"We have a lot to get even for, right?" I said quietly. Everyone nodded.

"You ready to be mean?" I said.

"She's sure mean," Danielle said.

I looked at Lisa and Leslie.

They were grinning and nodding at each other.

90

I leaned in close and for a long time, I whispered my plan.

When I was finished, everyone was laughing.

"Okay!" I said. "You guys have the popcorn, and we'll get plastic wrap."

But then I really felt bad. Plastic wrap is very bad for the environment. But just this once?

Anyway, for this project, we had to do it.

"It means we have to sneak back into school later," I said, looking first at Danielle, then at Leslie and Lisa. "And you know Fishface and the other teachers sometimes stick around. Does that scare you? It scares me."

"Yeah," Leslie said. "A little. But we're doing it anyway, right?"

"Right," Lisa said.

Danielle nodded.

"And Margaret?" I said. I looked over at her. She was at a desk up front, getting extra help from Fishface with her math homework. "She'll want to, too. But she'll be scared, big time."

"We'll ask her," Danielle said. "If she's too scared, she'll say so."

Then the bell rang, and everybody scooped up their books and papers, and we put our chairs up on our desks.

Michele was heading for the lockers at the same time as me, and I accidentally bumped her arm as we reached for our jackets.

It really was an accident, but she looked at me mad. "Why are you always so mean to me?" she said.

Me? To her?

"I'm sorry!" I said. "It was an accident!"

"Right," she said, real sarcastically.

"Really!" I said.

"Well, you're very mean," she said.

For just a minute, I felt bad. Maybe I *was* mean to her? Maybe if I was nice to her, she'd be nice to me?

Then I headed for the door with Danielle and Lisa and Leslie. But before we went out, all of us stopped at the door. Fishface has a new rule: each day we have to stop there before we go home and tell him one thing we liked about the day.

I usually just say that I'm glad the day is over.

That day, I said the usual.

Before I could get away, though, Fishface put a fishy hand on my arm. "You've never told me how you felt about your project with Michele," he said. "If you learned a lesson from it. Also, how's that worm project going?"

"It's going fine," I said, shaking off his hand.

"Tomorrow?" he said. "Plan on staying a while after class tomorrow to bring me up to date."

I rolled my eyes. "Yes, Mr. McGill," I said.

As we went outside, we heard Michele behind us. "This was a great day, Mr. McGill!" she said. "I'm so glad that Parents' Night is our school project. I know you think it's good. You give me so much support."

If I had any doubts about what we were about to do, they were gone then. Completely, absolutely gone.

Chapter 11

We raced to Leslie and Lisa's house and collected three huge bags full of popcorn. Then we went in the kitchen and snuck out three big rolls of plastic wrap from the pantry. And then we raced back to school.

First we hid the popcorn bags in the bushes, then walked slowly all the way around the school, real casually, as if we'd just come to play on the playground or something.

When we came around the side, we saw that there were only two cars in the teacher's parking lot — Mr. Knox's, the janitor's, and the art teacher's, old, deaf Mrs. Plotz. There was a third car, too, Fishface's car, over at the very edge of the regular parking lot near the woods. Fishface has a new red sports car — which seems weird since he is definitely the station wagon type. He always parks it far from the others, as if he's afraid it will catch dents or scratches from the other cars, the way people catch colds.

"Just three to watch out for," Danielle said.

"But one of them is Fishface!" Leslie answered.

"What difference?" Lisa said. "If we get caught, it doesn't matter who catches us."

"We're not getting caught," I said.

I hope.

Three cars — but we didn't see any other teachers or parents or anything.

We got the popcorn bags out of hiding and went around back.

The gym door was standing open, propped that way with a chair. Mr. Knox does that every day. "To air the place out from you stinky kids," he told me once, laughing — laughing, but I still think he meant it.

All five of us stood there, looking at the open door.

I wondered if the others were as nervous as me.

Margaret was sweating a lot, little beads of perspiration shining on her upper lip. Danielle was twisting a bit of hair around her finger. And Leslie and Lisa looked just normal.

"Ready?" Leslie said.

We all nodded, and Leslie led the way in, Lisa right on her heels, as if sneaking into school and sabotaging someone's locker was something they did every day.

I wondered if it was an act or if they were as scared as I was.

Inside, we could hear music playing loudly, coming from the direction of the cafeteria, a boom box, it sounded like. Probably Mr. Knox. Good! If he was in the cafeteria, he was far from the lockers, where we were going.

"Come on!" Leslie whispered over her shoulder. "Follow me."

She led the way to the lockers, the rest of us following.

Suddenly, Lisa went running past. "Race you!" she said.

And then Leslie took off, too. Their sneakers pounded the hall floor.

"I'm out of here!" Margaret said, turning back to the door.

Danielle put out a hand to stop her. "Wait!" she said.

I caught up to Leslie and Lisa. "Quit it, you two!" I said, glaring at them. "You want to get us all put in jail?"

"They don't put kids in jail," Lisa said. She was calmly opening Michele's locker, then Susan's locker.

Leslie bent over and started sorting through Michele's stuff. "Boy, she has enough lipstick and junk in here to be an Avon lady," she said softly. "And anyway, who's going to catch us? Fishface will be in the teachers' room. And there's nobody else but Mr. Knox and Plotz."

"Huh? What?" Lisa said, putting one hand up to her ear the way Plotz does.

"Pay attention," I said to them all. "Let's get this done. Now, start by tearing off a strip of plastic wrap."

"Wait!" Lisa said. "Incriminating evidence." She had taken a hairbrush from Susan's locker and was holding it up. "This good enough?" she asked.

I nodded.

"Okay," I said, "watch me." I picked up the plastic wrap. "Now, everybody, tear off a long strip."

We each took the plastic and tore off a long strip.

All the while, Margaret was looking around nervously.

I guess because she wasn't paying attention, her strip got stuck to her arm and then to itself.

"I'm stuck!" she whispered, picking at the strip that was all wound around her arm.

I sighed. "Tear off a new one," I said. "And hurry."

"Look at us!" Leslie said.

She and Lisa had a mess, plastic twisted all the way around their arms.

They were hysterical laughing.

"Will you quit it!" I said.

"Okay, okay," Lisa answered.

Only Danielle had a strip in her hands, one that wasn't stuck to something else.

Eventually, each person got a new, untwisted piece, and I showed them what to do. First, we took one strip and stretched it across Michele's open locker, down at the bottom, where you dump in shoes and books and all. We put several more strips over the first one to make sure it would stay. Then, when the space was tightly sealed, we poured the popcorn down behind it. When the popcorn reached the top of the strip, we tore off more strips and stuck them across the open locker and poured in more popcorn behind that. Plastic wrap and popcorn, plastic wrap and popcorn, all the way to the top. We filled the entire locker with popcorn, sealing it in.

You can put a *lot* of popcorn in just one locker.

When we were finished, we stood back, looking at it and smiling. And then Lisa stood on tiptoe, reached over the tiny opening we had left at the top, and dropped in Susan's hairbrush.

"Great!" I said.

"Perfect!" Danielle said.

"She deserves it!" Leslie answered.

She did.

And with just a little luck, tomorrow morning when Michele opened her locker door, the plastic wrap would come with the door — spilling out a ton of popcorn all over the hall.

"She's going to know it's us," Margaret whispered nervously. She was fighting with the plastic wrap again, trying to get it unwrapped from her arm. "Even with the hairbrush, she's going to know it's us."

"Me, maybe," I whispered back, "but not you."

"We could just tell her it was her popcorn balls that exploded," Lisa said.

Danielle laughed right out loud, then covered her mouth with her hand.

"How about we do her desk next?" Leslie said.

"Oh, yeah!" Lisa said. She looked at her sister. "Let's!"

The two of them started toward the stairs on tiptoe.

"Get back here!" I said. "You're going to get caught."

"Chicken!" Lisa said, not turning to look at us. She

wiggled her hips. "Bock, bock, bock!" she said over her shoulder.

"You'll be *fried* chicken!" I said. I was trying to whisper, but it's hard to yell and whisper at the same time. I followed them to the foot of the stairs. They had already gone up halfway. "Did you forget Fishface? And Plotz?" I hissed up at them. "The teachers' room is up there."

"Whoops!" Leslie said.

She and Lisa both started backing down the steps.

And then we heard it — footsteps in the hall above. Heavy footsteps.

Fishface footsteps? No, a kind of limping, heavy step.

Plotz!

We looked at each other.

"We're dead!" Margaret whimpered.

Danielle bent and grabbed the popcorn bags.

I picked up the boxes of plastic wrap.

And all five of us raced for the back door. Raced for it, feet pounding, not caring whether we made noise.

And when we got there — the door was shut. It wasn't propped open anymore!

Was it locked? Were we stuck?

Behind me, I could hear Margaret breathing hard, her breath coming in little gasps as though she was crying.

Leslie and Lisa were gasping, too, but whether they were crying or laughing I couldn't tell. But I thought I knew.

And Danielle was murmuring, "The stars! I knew it. We weren't alert enough."

And me, all I knew is I had to get out of here. I could feel my heart race wildly. I got to the door first and pushed the bar that was across the door.

Nothing.

Again, and still nothing. And then I practically threw myself against it, and the door opened. It was all right — it opened. And we were out of there.

Behind me, I could hear Margaret gasping, "The woods! Into the woods."

We raced across the parking lot, and in half a second, we had collapsed on the ground, hidden in the trees there.

Leslie and Lisa were hanging on to each other, holding each other up, they were laughing so hard.

Danielle was whispering something, thanking her lucky stars, I bet.

And I was looking at Fishface's car, right there at the edge of the woods. Looking at it and thinking. And thinking. And thinking. . . .

No, I told myself.

Yes.

No.

"I have to go home," Margaret said. "Okay? See you later? I have to recover."

"Yeah, we have to go, too," Lisa said.

"We have piano lessons at five," Leslie said. She turned to her twin. "I didn't practice. Will you pretend you're me and take both lessons? Miss McGraw won't know the difference."

"If you pay me," Lisa said.

They turned back to us. "Call you tonight," they both said then.

"See you," everybody said.

Margaret and Leslie and Lisa took off, leaving Danielle and me standing there. I was staring at that car.

"What?" Danielle said.

"His car," I said.

"What about it?" Leslie said.

"We could wrap it," I said.

"Wrap it in what?"

"Plastic. He'll never get it off!" I said.

"Won't it hurt it? Hurt the paint?" Danielle said.

"They use it on food."

She smiled. "He didn't let us vote for the project," she said.

"Right," I answered.

"We'd have to be fast," Danielle said.

"Very," I said.

"You wrap; I'll watch," she said. "I'll be the lookout."

And so I went to work.

I used up every last bit of the plastic wrap. Round and round, round and round the car I went, sealing it up so tight it would take weeks for it to come unwrapped. Windows, doors, everything. Round and round and round and round his car. The sun was beating down, and even as I put each piece on, I could feel it sealing up tight.

I had just finished the last roll when Danielle said, "Quit! He's coming!"

We dove back into the trees, crouching low, really

low, so low we were hidden by the weeds and branches.

We could see him coming from the school, sort of strolling across the parking lot, his lips pursed up in a fake whistle, as though he didn't have a care in the world. His one arm was loaded down with books, and he was bouncing car keys in the other hand.

It took a minute for him to notice.

Then he stopped. Frowned. Shook his head. Frowned some more. And then raced forward, papers trailing behind him as he ran.

He got to his car — and just stared. Stared. Shaking his head.

He put down his books, slowly, carefully, as if he was in a trance. Then he ran his hands over his car.

We were so close I could hear him swear.

Danielle was holding tight to my hand. Part of me wanted to laugh, but part of me was terrified, absolutely terrified.

After a minute, we saw him try to find the beginning of the wrapping — or the end — to unwrap. Then he gave up and pulled out a pocketknife and began hacking away at the wrapping.

Danielle and I tiptoed away, back through the trees, and ran for home. I didn't know about her, but I felt like I had to get home, inside, safe.

At the corner by the park, Danielle and I each called, "Bye," and she ran her way and I went mine.

I didn't bother to take the lucky way, the long way home. I was in too much of a hurry to care about superstition or good luck.

I took the shortcut, right through the park, right out onto High Street, and in a minute, I was home.

And I raced into the garden and hid behind a tree.

Because there, in front of my house, a car was parked. A sports car. A red sports car. A car that was wrapped and trailing yards and yards and yards of plastic.

Chapter 12

Some weird things happened after that, really weird. The first weird thing was that when Fishface finally came out of the house, he and Jake stood on the porch a long time, smiling and talking and even laughing.

Laughing?

And the second weird thing was that when Fishface was gone and I went in, Jake thought that what I had done was funny — that is, the part about the car. He didn't know yet about the locker. "Not nice," he kept saying, "but funny." But he did say he thought I should apologize.

Ha! Fat chance of that.

All night Jake just kept looking at me and laughing and shaking his head. "I'd hate to be on your wrong side, Brady Abbott," he said at supper that night.

Another weird thing was that the next day, Michele missed the hint about the hairbrush and blamed the popcorn all on me. But how could she prove it?

Danielle and Lisa and Leslie and Margaret, they all

swore that it must have been defective popcorn balls — that all of their popcorn balls had exploded at their homes. Mr. McGill said he was not going to get involved in placing blame — but since Michele had brought in the popcorn to begin with, she was responsible. And so Michele had to get a broom and clean it all up.

Nobody seemed to wonder where all that plastic wrap had come from.

But the thing that was really, really weird, was that Fishface didn't seem mad at me. What had he and Jake talked about? And why did Fishface keep looking at me as if he was waiting for something? An apology, like Jake had said? No way. Besides, he couldn't punish me. He could never prove it was me. In fact, he didn't say one single thing about it except that he liked meeting Jake.

Still, I had so many other things on my mind, that I couldn't let Fishface make me crazy. Saturday was coming. Saturday my dad would be here.

I didn't even know what I'd call him when I saw him. Dad. Daddy. My father. I tried all the words inside my head. I used to call him Daddy, but that was long ago, when I was little. And it seemed too intimate or something now, for a stranger. Well, not that he was a stranger exactly. But I didn't exactly know him, either.

And what would I say when I first saw him?

Hi, Dad. How are you?

No. Too boring, like talking to a pen pal.

Hi, Dad. I've missed you. Where have you been? Why didn't you write?

No! I would not.

That whole week, neither Jake nor I mentioned him again, as though we had made an agreement not to talk about it.

There was one good part of that week, though, and it was that Jake seemed better. He still had trouble with his breathing, but he seemed much stronger, and he got up every morning and worked a while in his garden. He even made dinner each night.

Finally it was Friday, the day before my dad was coming, and I still hadn't gotten up the courage to ask about him — when he was coming, what we were going to do, anything.

And then I had a thought: his bedroom! It was a mess. For years now, whenever we didn't know what to do with stuff, it ended up back there in Dad's room. Well, I'd just have to clean it up.

Or I could give up my room and sleep in the living room. There's a pullout couch there, and I've slept on it lots of times, when I've been sick and wanted to watch TV or something. That's what I'd do. So after school that Friday, I did a lot of cleaning up and vacuuming, and Jake didn't even have to tell me to do it.

Jake and I had just sat down to supper on Friday — fish cakes and macaroni and cheese and fried onions — when Jake said, "You've been awfully quiet all week."

"Well, you, too," I answered.

He nodded.

"Worried about tomorrow?" he asked.

"Not worried exactly," I said.

"What then?" Jake said.

What?

How could I tell Jake what I was thinking, tell him when I wasn't even sure myself?

Jake sighed and reached across the table for the salt and pepper.

I saw that his hand was shaking, shakier than I'd ever seen it.

"I asked you something last week," Jake said, and after he had snagged the pepper and brought it to his place, I noticed that he set it down without using it, burying his hand in his lap. "Had a purpose asking if you'd missed him all those years. Remember?" Jake went on.

I nodded.

"You weren't sure," Jake said.

Again I nodded.

"You figured that out yet?" he asked.

I frowned at him.

What a weird question! What difference did it make what I had felt for years? It was now that mattered.

But from the way Jake was looking at me, I could tell it mattered to him.

I shrugged. "No," I said. "I haven't figured it out. Why?"

"Just wondered," Jake answered. "You did — do — always look for those letters." He picked up the pepper and began sprinkling it heavily on his onions.

I tried not to look, to see if he was still trembling so much.

"So?" Jake asked. "If you've missed him, then you must . . . I guess I'm trying to figure out if you want to go live with him."

I looked up at him quickly.

He was still sprinkling pepper on his onions. Lots of it. The onions were almost black with pepper. And still he kept pouring it on, his head bent.

"Jake!" I said.

"What?" He looked up at me suddenly and stopped peppering his food.

"Nothing," I said.

Neither of us said anything for a long time.

My heart was racing so, I could hardly bear it. Go live with my dad? Not live here? Why not?

Jake made a face at his plate, then pushed the plate firmly away.

"Look!" he said, taking a deep breath. "You'll find out tomorrow, anyway, and it's better to hear it from me. He'll be here in the morning at nine. He's going to take you out with him, just for the day, just a visit — just a visit at first, before you all start living together. He'll take you to meet the others. There are others, you know."

"Others? Other what?"

"Children. Your father has other children."

Other children. My father has other children.

I stared at Jake. "He does?" I said. "He has? You mean, I have sisters? Brothers? Whatever?"

Jake nodded. "Half. Half brother, half sister."

Half. For one crazy minute, I pictured a child cut neatly in half, right down the middle, one eye, one arm, one leg. A half a sister, half a brother.

But of course I knew that wasn't what he meant. He meant my dad had married, had a new family.

A new family, a real family, just like I had always wanted to have. They were all together — the new family.

And Dad, he hadn't come to get me.

"How old?" I asked. "How old are the kids?"

"Two of them. One boy, one girl."

"How old?" I asked again.

"I was afraid you'd get in a tizzy about this," Jake said irritably.

"I'm not in a tizzy!" I said. "I just asked a question: How old are they?"

"Why don't you make us some coffee?" Jake said.

I got up and went to the stove. I got out the coffeepot and the coffee. Slowly, I poured in the water and measured the coffee.

"Four years old," Jake said to my back. "Four years old and one year old."

A four-year-old! A one-year-old? A *wife?* Where were they all going to fit? In Dad's room? We *had* to live here!

"Now, you can't go making a fuss about this," Jake said. "He married, he had children. Okay, so he didn't write or come back. It wasn't real nice of him, but it wasn't like he was abandoning you either. He knew you were all right. He knew you were cared for."

Cared for. That's what he used to say in his letters: "Take care of my girl."

"That's the first thing he asked when we talked," Jake went on. "He said, 'How's my girl?' That's exactly what he asked."

I turned to him. "He did?" I said. "You're not just making that up?"

"Now why would I do that?" Jake glared at me.

For a minute, I just looked back at him. And then I said, "Well, I think this stinks!"

Jake just shrugged. "It's life."

"Well, life stinks!" I said. "Him having a new *family* stinks!"

Jake held up a hand. "Now, listen, he's your dad. He married my daughter, and he gave me you, my granddaughter, so he can't be all that bad. And what'd you want him to do — be single the rest of his life? Just because he has other children is no reason to get all upset about it. He's still your dad, and a girl needs her —"

"Ha!"

"— dad, so don't go cutting off your nose to spite your face." He stopped then — another of his coughing fits.

When he was finished coughing, he blew his nose, then stuffed his handkerchief in his pocket. He did it all very deliberately and slowly, as though he was purposely taking his time.

After a while, he opened his mouth, then closed it, opened and closed it — while I just stared at him.

After a long time he spoke. "Your dad's a young man," he said. "I'm an old one."

"So?" I said. "I don't care!"

"Wait and see," Jake said.

I shook my head no.

But Jake said it again. "Wait and see," he said. "All right? Just wait and see. I think you'll like him, think you'll be happy."

Wait and see.

But I'd already been waiting a long time, waiting a long time to be part of a real family. And now, here was a real family, a ready-made real family.

And there must have been something wrong with me, because I felt anything but happy.

Chapter 13

Dad was coming next morning. And even though part of me was mad at him, partly, too, I couldn't help the racing of my heart.

I could hardly sleep that night. I had taken a bath before bed, and I even did my nails. My hair was easy to do: wash it and brush it. It was awfully short, little spikes all around my head. But it sure was easy.

I wondered if he'd like it.

I wondered if he could help Jake.

I wondered what he was like.

I wondered if he'd like . . . me.

I lay in bed, staring at the ceiling.

I knew I'd never get to sleep.

And then next thing I knew it was morning.

I sat up in bed and looked at the clock.

Six o'clock.

Three hours yet to wait.

I lay back down, but even though I worked at getting

comfortable, fluffing up the quilts and pillow, still I couldn't sleep.

Finally, I got up and dressed in my favorite jeans even though it wasn't even seven o'clock yet.

I got my favorite blue shirt and was going to take it out to the kitchen to iron it, but decided no. If I got out the iron, Jake would think I was making too much of this day. I never iron anything if I can help it.

What to do next?

I went back to my room, did my math homework, checked on my worms, and still it was only seven-fifteen.

In a little while, I heard Jake in the kitchen and smelled coffee brewing. I went out there with him.

He didn't look surprised to see me up so early.

He was wearing his old sweatshirt and the high-top sneakers.

I wondered if he did that on purpose, to show that my dad wasn't company or anything.

I also wondered if his heart was hammering as hard as mine.

But all he said was, "How about I cook you an omelet this morning?"

"With onions?" I said.

I meant it as a little joke, but Jake took me seriously.

"You want them?" Jake asked.

"No," I answered. "Just joking. Plain omelet would be good."

He didn't say anything more.

After a while, we both sat down to eat, and even

though both of us had plenty we could have said, neither of us said anything.

After we ate, I cleaned up the dishes while Jake went to the windowsill and began working on his herb garden, doing some plant cuttings and repotting.

At least he was pretending to work. But I noticed that he repotted the same plant three different times. He just kept switching it from one pot to the next and then back again. He'd wear it out if he didn't leave it alone. But I knew, too, that he didn't want me to tell him that.

I finished the dishes, then went to the bathroom and brushed my teeth.

I stood there in the bathroom for a minute, looking at myself in the mirror, pretending to be my dad seeing me for the first time in a long time.

What would he see?

Blue eyes, kind of nice, with little streaks in them, like stars.

A skinny face. A pointy chin. Freckles.

And a long neck! Man, I have a long neck! How come I never noticed that before?

I pulled up the collar of my shirt.

Then I smiled at myself in the mirror, pretending I was smiling at Dad.

What a stupid smile I have! How come I never noticed that before either? It's really dumb-looking! Kind of half a smile, as if I'm afraid to smile right out.

I smiled wider.

Gross. I looked like a horse. All that showed was teeth and gums.

I tried tipping my head to one side, looking upward, blinking and smiling the way Michele does.

Oh, bluck!

I just shook my head, then went back to my room. I made my bed, brushed my hair once more, and went back to the kitchen.

Then to the porch.

Then to the living room.

Back to my room.

And then, finally, it was nine o'clock. Nine o'clock — he was coming.

And then it was nine-fifteen.

Nine-thirty.

Where was he?

I looked out the front window for a moment, then went back to the kitchen. Jake was still there, really wrecking his little herb garden.

I stood behind him, watching him for a moment, my hands behind my back, tipping up and down from my toes to my heels. "Why don't you leave those alone?" I said.

"Why don't you mind your own business?" Jake answered.

"Just thought you might like to know you're wrecking them," I said.

I went to the living room and turned on the TV.

I went all around the channels, but nothing. Geez! What stupid programs are on on Saturday. You have to be six years old to enjoy Saturdays.

Nine-forty-five.

At ten o'clock, I started looking out the window, watching for strange cars coming down the street.

But then I realized that there are always strange cars coming down the street, so how would I know which was his?

Maybe I'd see him walking up to the house, or else walking up the block, looking for the house. Would he remember where it was?

I gave up, came back, and sat on the couch.

After a little while, Jake came in from the kitchen. He picked up his quilt from the back of the chair and sat down heavily in the rocker, not looking at me. He picked up the sewing basket, chose some thread, and went to work.

I watched his needle go in and out of the fabric, in and out, in and out. Jake was jerking the needle angrily. He's usually much more careful and neat about his sewing.

He was going to tear the fabric if he wasn't more careful.

I kept checking my watch. At first, my watch was going too slow, and then it was going too fast. Because by then it was ten-forty-five and he still wasn't there.

I never saw Jake even once look at his watch, but he kept making that annoying clicking sound that he makes when he's disapproving of something.

I wished he'd *stop* that!

Ten-fifty.

Maybe he was lost. Did he remember how to get here? It had been a long time, and things change, like the landmarks had changed. Maybe that was it. The grocery store at the corner was gone, and there was a bank there now and . . .

That had to be it. He was lost, and I bet he'd been trying to call but our phone was accidentally off the hook, not pressed down hard enough to keep the button down. That had happened before, when a pencil got stuck under it.

I went to the kitchen where the phone is. The phone looked okay — nothing keeping it off the hook, not even a little. But just to be sure it was working, I picked it up to listen, trying to be very quiet so Jake wouldn't know.

There was a dial tone, and quietly, I put the phone down.

But then I thought, What if he had tried to call at that exact moment and got a busy signal? But he'd call back; I knew he would.

I went back in the living room and sat down.

And then I heard a car door slam, right outside on the street.

I looked at Jake. He was sitting there so still he was surely holding his breath, staring down at the quilt in his hands.

"Jake?" I said.

"What?"

"Get it, okay?"

He looked up from his sewing and shook his head no.

I motioned to him, then pointed to the door. "Go!" I said. But my voice came out squeaky, just barely a whisper. "Go!" I said louder. "Answer the door. Please?"

"You go," he said. "It's you he's coming for."

"But —"

"Don't fret," Jake said calmly. "He'll like you just fine."

Would he? Even with my hair like this? My long neck? My stupid smile? I wanted to run and hide. If the bell hadn't rung at that exact moment, I might have, too.

But it did ring, and I had no choice. I went and opened the door.

And there, on the porch, was a man I had never seen before.

He was tall and thin and very good-looking, better looking than Mr. Godwin even. He was wearing a leather jacket open over a sweater, and his hair was long and curling around his ears.

His face was tanned, with two deep creases on either side of his mouth, smile lines like.

He was wearing beat-up jeans, but just kind of worn, not the kind you deliberately put holes in. And there were sunglasses dangling from a cord around his neck.

Was this my dad?

But it couldn't be my dad! He didn't look like I remembered him at all.

Until he spoke.

"It's her," he said softly. "It's her at last. All grown up. My girl."

His girl.

My dad.

He was reaching for me, both arms held wide. I remembered something then, something from long, long ago, something I had completely forgotten till that very moment: he used to hold his arms wide just like that. "Run and I'll swing you!" he'd say. And I'd come running down the block to him and run right into his arms. He'd grab me up and swing me around, around, and around, high in the air.

Now his arms were held wide to me again.

But I didn't run into them.

I just stood there watching him, watching him take the next step from the porch to the house, his arms still open wide, his smile still wide.

A nice smile, not a simpy one like mine.

Then he was real close, and he wrapped his arms around me, and I let him.

"My girl," he whispered. "It's my girl."

Chapter 14

Dad said hi to Jake, then bye to him, and we left in a hurry. Both Dad and Jake seemed anxious, like strange cats in a room together. Dad especially acted as if he wanted to quick get away.

I knew that they had talked on the phone, and I couldn't help wondering how that had gone. They acted very strange together.

I wondered if my dad was feeling what I was feeling. Because even though Jake had said last night that I should understand that Dad had his own life to live, I had a feeling Jake wasn't so understanding himself.

Dad's car was parked right outside, a small black car, new, but kind of dusty and dirty. The inside was dirty, too, with old toys and pieces of burst balloons and some McDonald's cups on the floor. There was a sprinkling of what looked like salt on my side of the seat, and some dried-up french fries.

Dad looked apologetic when I brushed off the salt. "I know," he said as he started up the car. "Looks terrible, doesn't it? But it's hard to keep a car clean when you have kids, you know?"

No. I didn't know. I'd never had kids, and Jake and I didn't even have a car. But I nodded, anyway.

We pulled out into the street.

"Where are we going?" I asked.

"I'm going to take you to meet my family — your family. Would you like that?"

He turned and looked at me for a moment, but turned away quickly without waiting for my answer. "They've been so excited about meeting you," he said. "William has been. He's the oldest. Susanna, she's too young to know yet. A pretty baby, almost as pretty as you."

I didn't say anything. I didn't know if I wanted to meet them. They'd been living with him all those years, and I hadn't. And I didn't know yet what I felt about that.

Dad put one arm along the back of the seat. "So," he said. "Have you missed your old dad, Brady?"

"Yes," I said, because suddenly I knew that was the truth, and I wondered what Jake would think about that.

"Did you think of me?" Dad asked.

"Yes."

All the time at first. Why didn't you write? But of course I didn't say that out loud.

"I missed you, too," Dad said. "Every once in a

while, I'd just be working or something, and you'd pop into my head, just like that."

"I used to think you were in jail," I said suddenly.

"You did!" He turned to me, surprised looking. "Now why would you think that?"

But I just shook my head. I couldn't tell him the real reason — that if he was in jail, that would be a good reason for not writing, that maybe the only reason he didn't write was because he wasn't allowed to write.

For a while, we drove silently.

I kept sneaking looks at him, trying to see if he seemed the way he used to be. But it was hard to tell. I didn't really remember the way he used to be. I remembered only that there were times, weeks it seemed, when he hardly spoke to me at all, when he'd sit staring at the TV, even when it wasn't on. And then weeks when he'd act really friendly, too friendly, so much so that it was scary almost. It used to be confusing to me. We were living with Jake at the time, and Jake explained it was because of the war — that something had happened to Dad during the war that made him like that. But that confused me, too, because I hadn't even been born when Dad was in Vietnam, so I didn't see why that still bothered him so much.

Anyway, I couldn't remember him much, so sitting beside him then, I couldn't tell if he was the way he used to be or not. Only thing I could tell was that he seemed much older — that I was sure of. Or maybe it was that I was older. We couldn't really talk all that much about Matchbox cars anymore.

"You mad at me?" he asked after a while.

"No!" I said. "No! Why?"

"Because you're not talking to me."

"I'll talk," I said. "I just . . . I just don't know what to say, what to talk about."

"Say anything. Talk to me about you. Anything you want to say."

He had a funny way of talking, super fast, clipping off each word as if he had to hurry on to the next one.

I didn't know how to answer him. How could I catch him up with all those years?

"I'm . . . well, I'm fine," I said. "I like school. Except our teacher's kind of weird. I'm on a Save the Earth project. Sort of like your Save the Whales, remember?" But Dad just shrugged and smiled without answering.

"And I have lots of friends, lots of friends," I rushed on. "Do you remember Danielle?"

"No," Dad said. "But I'm sure you have lots of friends. Boyfriends, too, I bet."

"No way!" I said.

He frowned. "You're just saying that," he said.

"Not really," I said.

"Oh," he said.

I thought he seemed disappointed so I made one up, right on the spot. "There's . . . Jason!" I said quickly.

To myself, I said, Jason Marks, *not* Jason Cavanaugh.

"Ah-hah!" he said. "I thought so. Lucky Jason. I'm going to have to check him out, to be sure he's all right for my girl."

My girl. His girl. Me.

I smiled.

Dad took his hand off the back of the seat then and used both hands to turn the wheel. He turned the corner so sharply that I slid over against the door, and then he made another sharp turn and we were in the parking lot of a diner, the Duchess Diner. It's where everybody at school goes with their parents, after skating parties or after school concerts and stuff.

Dad pulled up near the door, parked, and then turned to me.

"Hungry?" he asked.

I wasn't at all. I was too nervous. But I nodded because eating would give us something to do while we got to know each other.

He turned off the car, opened his door, and got out. He practically ran around to my side to open the door for me. He took my arm, held the door while I got out, and closed the door, and then, still holding my arm, we went up the steps to the diner.

I should have felt like a movie star, but for some reason, I didn't. I wasn't even sure if I hoped my friends would be there, if I wanted them to see me with him or not.

Inside, Dad took a quick look around, then led the way past the booths to a table in back where he stopped.

There was a little boy there, wearing a green T-shirt. With him was a pretty, thin woman with huge dark eyes. She had a baby on her shoulder, and she was patting the baby's bottom in a kind of rhythm, soft and sweet. She smiled up at us as we came near.

"Daddy!" the boy yelled. "I want chocolate milk, and Mom wouldn't let me. Say yes, please? Pleeeease?"

He slid off his chair and grabbed Dad's leg, as if he would climb right up it.

Dad bent and picked the kid up, holding him up right at shoulder level. "Brady," he said, "this is your brother, William. Willie, this is Brady."

William was not my brother. He was a half brother. A half brother who lived with his dad. My dad.

"Are you a boy or a girl?" Willie said to me.

"Will-*ie!*" his mother said.

"I'm a girl!" I said, glaring at him.

"Oh," William said. "How come your hair's like that?"

I shrugged.

"Sit down, sit down, everyone," Dad said, and he pulled over some more chairs, and we all sat.

"Well, hello, Brady," the woman said to me, and she smiled. "What a cute little thing you are."

"This is Marlene," Dad said to me. "My wife. Or maybe you'll want to call her Mom. And that's our baby, Susanna. How's that for a pretty name for a pretty baby?"

Call her Mom? She wasn't my mom, not any more than Willie was my brother.

Suddenly Susanna started to scream. She closed her eyes and her face got all scrunched up and she turned practically purple.

Marlene bounced her around a bit and continued to smile at her and pat her.

"Hungry, Brady?" Dad said. "What can I get you?"

"I wanna go!" Willie said. "We were waiting a long time."

"Well," Dad said, "if you've waited a long time, I guess you can wait a little longer."

Dad turned to me. "What do you want?" he asked, and he was talking again in that super-fast way. "Anything at all," he said. "Steak and eggs? Hamburger and fries? A shake? What? I'm having the hamburger special — that looks good to me. What do you want, huh?"

"Chocolate milk!" Willie said.

Dad shook his head. "Not you. Brady. So what for you, Brady?"

"Just a Coke," I said.

"Oh, come on, now!" Dad said. "You can do better than that. How about a bagel and cream cheese? Bagel and cream cheese is always good, right? Or maybe you want lox and a bagel?"

"No, thanks," I said.

"What about a piece of pie, then? They have good —"

"Bill," Marlene said, quietly. "She said just a Coke."

She and Dad exchanged looks, and she put a hand over Dad's.

Dad shrugged.

"Okay, okay, a Coke it is," he said.

The waitress came over, and Dad ordered: the hamburger special for him and a Coke for me. Willie ordered plain milk — he made a disgusting face when he said that — and an egg salad sandwich. Marlene ordered black coffee and whole wheat toast with jelly, no butter.

When the waitress was gone, we all sat there looking at each other — all of us except for Susanna, who wasn't looking at anyone. She still had her eyes screwed tightly closed and she had begun screaming her head off again.

Suddenly I thought I knew just how the baby felt: miserable. I even thought everyone else looked pretty miserable, too.

Willie was sulking about his chocolate milk, his bottom lip stuck out, his eyebrows pulled in together in a major pout.

Marlene was frowning, chewing on the inside of her cheek, and looking off into the distance.

And Dad seemed almost frantic.

"So!" he said. "So this is my little family, all together at last. What fun, right? It's been so long. So long. So what should we do today?" He was rubbing his hands together. "What do you say we go to the park? Or go see the house. Would you like to see our house?"

"We have a room ready for you," Marlene said quietly, but she didn't look at me.

A room? They didn't really think I was going to live there, did they?

"Right!" Dad said. "Would you like to see your room? It's all pink. We decided a girl likes pink. Wait till you see it. You do like pink, don't you?"

I wanted to say, "Dad?" — or something — just to hush him up. But I couldn't get the word *Dad* out. I could say it in my head, but not out loud. I also had other things to say, like, What about Jake? Did they have his room ready, too?

I didn't say any of that, though.

Instead, I just said, "Uh . . ." and after a moment, Dad looked at me.

And then I blurted out something, something I hadn't planned to say at all. "Are you still a doctor?" I said. "I mean, I know you did doctoring stuff. In the war. But are you retired or something?"

He and Marlene exchanged looks again.

Dad got very still. "No," he said. "I don't do that kind of thing anymore."

"Does that mean you're not a doctor?" I said.

"Not a doctor. Never have been. Just a medic, once upon a time. So what about going to our house? You're going to love your room."

"But you still know about doctoring?" I persisted. "How to do it?"

Dad looked angry for some reason. Or maybe it was just upset.

I could feel my face get red. Jake would have a conniption fit if he knew what I was about to say. But I had to do it.

"Can you look at Jake when we get back?" I asked.

"What's the matter with Jake?" Dad asked.

"You know. Same thing he's had forever. His lungs?"

"Oh, that." Dad shrugged.

"Who's Jake?" Willie interrupted. "Is he the one who called us?"

Dad nodded.

Willie looked at me. "You're going to come live with us, right?"

I started to answer, but Willie added something. "You have to, right?" he said. "You have to come 'cause Jake doesn't want you 'cause he's going to die, right?"

"Will-*ie!*" his mother said. She reached and grabbed him by the arm. "Now, you hush!" she said, and she glared at him.

He yanked away from her hand and glared back.

For a long minute, no one spoke. Even Susanna was suddenly quiet.

"Jake's got emphysema," Dad said into the silence. "A little dose of oxygen occasionally would help him. But he'll never get all better."

Oxygen . . . He'll never get all better. . . .

My heart was thumping so hard, so violently in my throat, that I was sure suddenly that I was going to throw up. I swallowed hard, trying to force down that feeling.

You have to come with us 'cause Jake's going to die.

Marlene stood up, bouncing the baby on her shoulder. "I'll take her outside," she said. "Leave you all to get acquainted."

"Your breakfast is here!" Willie said.

"It's okay," she said. "I'm not really hungry after all."

She pulled a blanket around Susanna. "She's only

happy when she's moving," she said, smiling. "A lot like her dad."

And then she left and as soon as she started walking, Susanna stopped yelling.

In the silence, I looked at my dad, at Willie.

At this family.

This was my family. Or was it?

Chapter 15

When we finished and went outside, Dad put Susanna into a little car-seat thing between him and Marlene in the front of the car, and Willie and I climbed in the back.

"I get a window!" Willie yelled.

"Duh!" I muttered to him. "There are two windows."

He made a face at me.

If this is what it was like to have a brother, I didn't think I wanted one.

"Where are we going?" I said to Dad as he started the car.

"Home," Dad said. "Want to see your home?"

"We're moving soon, maybe," Willie said. "To California."

"Right," I said.

"We are, right, Dad?" he said.

"Well," Dad said. "Maybe, maybe not. But for now,

we're showing Brady our new house. That okay with you, Brady?"

"Yes," I said.

What else could I do?

Dad turned from the parking lot out onto the highway, and practically the minute the car was moving, Willie fell asleep — which was fine with me.

After a minute, Dad and Marlene started talking very quietly, and I heard them say my name. Even though I strained to hear what it was they were saying about me, I couldn't. They were talking just too quietly.

And then, I must have fallen asleep just like Willie, because next thing I knew, we had turned off the highway and the car was bouncing along a bumpy road and we were there.

I sat up, and Willie woke up, too. We were coming up a long, rutted driveway to a house, a nice sprawly white house, sitting on a little hill. There was a new lawn in front and a little fence around the lawn.

"It's not very big," Marlene said, looking at me over the back of the seat. "But I think you'll like it."

"I get the swing!" Willie yelled. "I get the swing!"

Who wanted his swing?

As soon as Dad stopped the car, Willie jumped out and raced for the swing set.

The swing set was shiny and new, a brilliant bluish green. In fact, everything about the house was new, as if it had all been built yesterday. But it was a real house where a real family lived. Maybe it wouldn't be so bad here. And I bet Jake would love it. Nothing had been planted yet, and Jake would have a whole new garden to create.

I followed Dad up the steps, Marlene beside me, carrying Susanna, who was asleep.

"Come on in!" Dad said. "Welcome home!"

Dad opened the front door into a small, bright living room crammed with furniture and toys. Everything looked brand new, except for the toys. The biggest thing in the room was a TV. I wondered if he still got in those moods where he just sat and stared at the TV.

"Living room!" Dad said, with a wave of his hand. Then he said, "Follow me!"

He led the way down a small hall.

Marlene stayed in the living room with the baby, and I followed Dad down the hall.

"Kitchen!" he said, waving a hand to the right off the hallway.

I looked. A small room, all black and white: white tiles on the walls and black and white tiles on the floor and one entire wall made of glass bricks. Even the tables and chairs repeated the black-and-white theme, with cushions that were spotted like the black and white spots on a cow.

Wow! A cool, modern kitchen!

There was an open can of cat food on the floor, half of it gone, the remaining half dried up and stiff.

Cats! They had a cat! But my gerbils . . . And what about Roxy? I'd have to leave Roxy!

"We'll get this mess cleaned up in a jiff," Dad said,

nodding at the food on the kitchen floor. "We were just in a hurry this morning to come see you."

He moved away from the kitchen and waved a hand to the other side of the hall. "Bedrooms," he said.

Then he waved to the end of the hall. "And the bath!" he said. "And your room. And that's it. Not too bad, huh? We just moved in a few months ago, but we won't be here much longer, I don't think, maybe get a bigger place now that you're with us. Still, who knows?"

From the hall, I could see into the bedrooms.

One was clearly Dad's — his and Marlene's.

The other one was for kids.

There was a kid's bed against one wall, with railings on the outside side and a bedspread that had designs painted on it so it made the bed look like a car. There was a crib against the other wall and between them about a zillion toys flung around on the floor.

"Come on," Dad said. "Let's see your room."

He led the way to a room at the end of the hall and flung open the door.

It was really tiny, hardly bigger than a big closet. But everything in it seemed to fit so well, almost as if each piece was specially designed for it, like a dollhouse. There was a tiny desk fitted in between the two windows, and under one of the windows was a window seat. There was a narrow white high-poster bed against the other wall, with a very stiff-looking mattress, covered with a pink fluffy bedspread. There was a tiny white dresser next to the bed of matching white wood. The whole room was very frilly, not at all like what I was used to, and not a thing was out of place. The whole thing looked as if it had been lifted right out of a Sears catalog, right down to the old-fashioned hat hanging on one of the bed posters.

Dad smiled at me. "Like it?" he asked.

I nodded and tried to look happy. I mean I was happy. But I also definitely felt a little weird.

"I'm glad you're here," Dad said.

I heard the baby start crying again, and Dad headed back for the living room.

"Make yourself at home!" he called over his shoulder.

In a minute, I heard sounds of a baseball game coming from the TV.

I looked around me. Make myself at home. But it wasn't home.

There weren't even any books here.

And the bed, it was all frills! It didn't look like the kind you could just sit on without getting in trouble.

I crossed the room to the window and looked out.

Still, spring was coming, and Jake could plant. . . .

But wait a minute! Where was Jake's room?

Dad stuck his head back in the door. "Brady?" he said. "How would you like to go to a movie tonight? Your mom and I, we'll take Susanna and see one movie, and you can go right next door — it's one of those twin theaters — and see a Disney movie with Willie. Would you like that?"

A Disney movie? With Willie? That didn't sound like a great night.

"Yes?" Dad was smiling at me. "No?"

"I don't know," I said. "I mean, I haven't had a chance to talk to you. A movie . . ."

"Oh, Brady!" Dad said. "We haven't had any time together, have we, with the kids around and all? We will, though, I promise — we'll have lots of time. Tell you what, you and me, we'll take a little walk in just a while, just the two of us, just as soon as this ball game's over. Okay?"

I nodded.

"So I'll tell Marlene and Willie yes about the movie, okay? I knew I could count on you."

Count on me.

"Dad?" I said. "Where's Jake's room?"

"Jake's room? What do you mean?"

"His room. You know. Where's he going to sleep?"

Dad scratched his neck. "Well, when he visits, I guess he can . . . Don't worry. We'll make room for him."

When he *visits?*

Then a phone was ringing somewhere, and Dad went to answer it.

In a minute, he was back in the doorway. "For you," he said. "In the kitchen."

"Me?" I said.

"Jake," Dad said. "Checking up, I bet."

Jake!

I raced out of the room and into the kitchen — and almost stepped on a fat gray cat that streaked out the door as I came in.

The phone was over against the wall, and I picked it up.

135

"Hello?" I said.

"Brady!" Jake said in that raspy, breathless voice. "You all right?"

No. But I couldn't speak. My heart. Or something. Something hurt in my chest. Maybe it was my lungs — maybe I had the same thing wrong that Jake did. Because even though I tried to speak, no sound came out.

"Brady?" Jake said again. "You there? You all right?"

"No." I managed to get the word out. "No."

"What?" Jake said. "Speak up. I can't hear you."

"No," I whispered again, then cleared my throat. "I want to come . . ."

"What?" he said.

I had to force the word past the lump in my throat. Force it.

"Home," I whispered. "I want to come home."

Chapter 16

I went back to Jake's that night, although it was very late by the time we started out — late because it was after midnight when we all got back from the movie.

Dad wanted me to stay over, but I told him I hadn't brought any stay-over stuff, which was true.

But more than that, I just had to get away from there. I had to get home to my own room. I needed to be in my own room and my own bed. At least for now.

It took over an hour to get back, and all the way there, I barely spoke. My dad didn't notice, though. He just talked and talked, his voice racing along, and I heard some of what he said, and some I tuned out completely. He told me all about the movie they had seen, every detail of the plot. And then he told me all about building his house, and about the kind of lumber they used and how he was a builder now, how much he liked doing that. He told me lots of other things. Lots and lots of things. But not one word about why he had never come back for me. I knew then that he had never wanted me or he'd have come for me. We couldn't have driven more than an hour to get to his house. He could have come for me easily, or at least come to see me, a zillion times over the years. If he had wanted to.

But then why had he come for me now?

Only because Jake called him, told him he had to come.

When Dad dropped me off at Jake's and I got out of the car, Dad called after me, "See you next weekend! Or else the weekend after! And we'll make definite plans, okay?"

I waved back but didn't answer.

I went up the steps and into the house.

Jake was sitting right where I had left him that morning, in the big red armchair, his sewing stuff still on his lap.

He looked tired, deep lines around his mouth, his eyes red-rimmed as if he had been fighting off sleep.

He looked at his watch. "Well, you're late enough!" he said. He said it real mad-like, as if it were my fault.

I just shrugged.

"How'd it go?" Jake asked then, a kind of hesitation in his voice. "You like your dad all right? You sounded upset on the phone."

"It was all right," I said. I didn't look at him. "I'm going to bed now."

I went through the living room, right past Jake's chair, then out the other door, the one that leads to the hall. I went down the hall to my room.

But when I reached my door, I stopped, thinking. I had never, never, never gone to bed without kissing Jake good night. Even when we had fights, and we had plenty of fights, I always kissed him good night.

But not tonight. I could not. I was so angry at him. But why? He hadn't done anything.

Not anything but found my dad. And he had even asked me, he had said, You sure you want to find him?

I took a deep breath, went in my room, and closed my door. Then I went over to the dresser and leaned over close to the mirror, looking at myself.

Was I really pretty, like my dad had said?

Jake had never told me that.

Jake never gives me a compliment, not ever.

Stupid old man! Why was he sick? Why did he find my dad? Why was he sending me to that awful, frilly, stupid place?

That wasn't real family.

Why hadn't I known before what I knew now?

Suddenly I flung myself down on the bed, facedown, burying my face in my pillow.

But I did not cry. I did not. I would not.

If Jake died, I'd make out somehow. It wouldn't be that long till I was grown up, or at least till I was old enough to live alone, anyway. Maybe I'd even run away.

A part of me said this was stupid, that if I didn't want to go, I didn't have to go.

But then what had I been waiting for all these years?

But then I had a different thought: maybe Jake wasn't much sicker than he'd always been. It was just that these spells that came once in a while, they'd been coming more often lately. So what? We'd lived through them before.

Still, my head hurt from thinking.

I rolled over on my back, but I kept the pillow over my face.

I kept thinking that I had to get up, go to the bathroom, wash my face, put on my pajamas, pull up the covers. But I could hardly move, my head hurt so.

After a while, I took the pillow off my face and tucked it under my head. I reached out and switched off my lamp so it wouldn't hurt my eyes. I'd get up and go brush my teeth in a minute.

But I must have fallen asleep, because I woke up and heard someone moving around in the room.

Willie!

What was he doing in here?

I was just about to sit up, to say, "Get out of here, Willie!"

But then I realized that I must have been dreaming. It wasn't Willie, and I wasn't at my dad's house. I was in my room at home. And it was Jake in my room — Jake, stiff and awkward, but moving as softly around the room as though he were a shadow. I saw him open one of my windows and stand there a while, looking out at the night. A breeze blew in, making the shade flap softly for a moment. Jake put up a hand and stilled it, and still stood looking out, his face turned up to the stars.

I lay watching him, wondering what he was doing, what he was thinking, why he was there.

He hardly ever came in my room, except when I was sick or something.

After a moment, he moved from the window to the bed.

I squeezed my eyes almost shut, leaving them open just a crack, just enough to see between my eyelashes, to actually *see* my eyelashes, see them moving across my vision like tiny blades of grass. I breathed softly, slowly, pretending to be asleep.

Then Jake was pulling the covers up and tucking them around my shoulders, saying something, something soft, something I couldn't make out.

I continued to breathe deeply, pretending sleep.

Don't go, Jake, don't go.

And then he brushed his hand so gently across my forehead — his cold, tough old hand.

It took all my concentration to hold back the tears.

Why didn't you tell me my dad was a jerk? Why didn't you tell me he doesn't really want me?

But I didn't cry. And he didn't move away — for a long, long time, he didn't move.

Why didn't you tell me that this is home? Why didn't you tell me that you are my home?

Chapter 17

The next few days were weird. Jake didn't ask any more how things went, or what my dad had said or done or anything. And I didn't offer anything. But Jake seemed to be watching me all the time. I'd look up from reading or watching TV or something, and he'd be looking at me. Sometimes, he'd raise his eyebrows as if he were asking a question, but always I looked away.

What was he asking? And what could I tell him? What could I say? That it had all turned out differently from what I had hoped? That it was all his fault? It wasn't his fault.

Still . . .

And it was weird, but when Monday came, the same kind of thing seemed to be happening at school. Fishface kept looking at me, but not in that mean way he had so often, as if he was challenging me about something. This was more as if he was waiting for me to say something, too.

And the days were racing by, and Parents' Night was coming. And I didn't know at all how I felt about that.

Even Danielle was acting weird. For two days now, she had kept looking as if she was about to say something, opening her mouth, then closing it. And then she'd stop and look away.

So what was bugging them all? All I knew was that I had a million things on my mind. No, not a million. Two.

Jake. And my dad.

And I had no idea what I was going to do about either one of them.

It was just a few days before Parents' Night, and Danielle and I were walking home to her house, when she tucked her arm through mine, the way she does sometimes.

"Brady?" she said just as we came around the corner in front of her house. "I have to tell you something before we go in."

"Uh-oh," I said. "Trouble."

"How do you know that?" she said.

I shrugged. "You don't have to be a genius to know that. When anybody starts with 'I have to tell you something,' it's always trouble."

She sighed and sat down on her front steps, and I sat down beside her.

"You're going to be awfully mad," she said. "Or upset. But it wasn't my fault. Honest."

"What wasn't your fault?" I said.

She sighed and ran a finger back and forth over the

stuff between the bricks. "You know that little plastic ball, the one the gerbils run around in?"

"You broke it?" I said.

"No . . . not that," she said.

"What then?" I said. "What did you break?"

She shook her head. And she looked absolutely miserable. "Nothing," she said. "But something . . . broke itself," she said.

"Broke itself?" I said.

"Uh-huh. Jelly," she said.

"Jelly? My gerbil?" I turned and stared at her. "She's getting better, right? Her tail was all healed up!"

Danielle kept running her fingers over the bricks. "Well, not really. See, yesterday, she was playing in that ball. And then I looked at her, and suddenly, she was just lying there. And she didn't move. And I —"

"Yesterday?" I said. "She's been lying there since yesterday?"

"No, not since yesterday. She's not there anymore."

"What do you mean? What are you talking about?"

"I threw her away."

"You threw her away!?"

She nodded. "She's dead," she said.

For a long time, I didn't say anything.

"Well, it wasn't my fault!" Danielle said.

"And you didn't even tell me?" I said.

"I'm telling you now!"

"And you just threw her away?"

"Well, what did you want me to do? Leave her there in the little ball? She was dead!"

Suddenly I could feel tears welling up. I wanted to scream, but instead, I was crying.

I just looked at Danielle, the tears pouring down my face.

"The least you could have done was bury her!" I said. "Where did you throw her?"

"In the trash," she said, and the tears were running down her face, too. "Around back."

I jumped up and raced around back of the house to where they keep the trash pails.

I could hear Danielle's feet pounding behind me, following me.

I pulled the lid off the first pail. It was empty.

I took the other lid off. That was empty, too.

Danielle was just standing there watching me.

Trash day. Today was trash pickup day. I couldn't even bury her.

"You're so mean!" I said to Danielle. "You are *so* mean!"

And I turned and ran.

I ran and ran and ran. But I didn't run home.

I started off toward the park, and then I ran through the park and I kept on going. I didn't know where I was going, and I didn't care. I just had to run.

I ran until I couldn't make myself run anymore, and then I sat down on a curb and caught my breath, and then I stood up and started walking.

I walked and walked.

It began to get dark, and still I walked.

I kept going until I was in a part of the town I didn't recognize, places I had never seen before.

145

But still I walked.

Maybe I'd walk until — what?

By then, though, it was darker, and I started to get worried.

I wasn't really running away. I was just running.

And now I was tired and scared. So I turned around and started back the way I'd come.

I had no idea how far I had come, but it took a long time to finally find a place that seemed familiar.

Finally I was at an intersection where lots of cars were going by, and then I saw the crossover to the highway, and I knew where I was. But it took at least another half hour before I was in my own neighborhood, and by then it was totally dark.

Jake would be having a conniption fit.

When I finally turned the corner and could see my house, I saw that all the lights were on, streaming out onto the sidewalk in front. And when I got closer, I could see Jake standing at the front door.

I took a deep breath.

He'd start to yell, and I was ready to yell back.

But when Jake saw me, he didn't yell.

All he did was hold the door open wide, and I came in.

And then he did something he'd never done before — or at least not in so long that I couldn't even remember.

Before I was even fully inside, he reached out to me. He reached out and pulled me in close to him, so close I was held tightly against his chest, so close I couldn't pull away even if I tried.

And I didn't feel like trying. I was too tired to pull away.

Jake held me tightly in both arms, rocking me a little, back and forth, back and forth. And then he lay his head atop my head. And I began to cry.

I cried and I cried.

Jake led me to a chair. He sat down, and then, as if I were just a little baby, he pulled me into his lap.

For a very long time we sat like that, me crying, Jake saying, "There, there."

I don't know how long we sat like that. But finally, finally, I had cried enough. Enough tears for my gerbil. Enough tears for my dad.

When I finally took a long, shaky breath, Jake said, "Hungry? Supper's been ready a long time."

"Sort of hungry," I said.

I was hungry, but funny, I didn't want to get out of his lap. I'm much too big to be sitting in his lap, I knew. But it felt good all the same.

Anyway, I stood up and both of us went out to the kitchen.

When we finally sat down and it was time for the prayer, Jake took my hand and held it, the way we always do. But he held it extra long before letting go.

We ate silently — chicken-something-or-other, loaded with onions.

I didn't eat much, though. It wasn't that it wasn't good. It was good enough in spite of all the onions. I guess I just wasn't as hungry as I'd thought I was.

Jake didn't seem hungry either, because he was just pushing the food around, taking a little bite, then putting the fork down, then picking it up again. Maybe there were too many onions even for him.

Finally Jake put down his fork and said, "Maybe I made a mistake."

I looked at him.

"In sending for your father," he added.

I waited a very long time, but Jake didn't speak again. He was turning his fork over and over — tines up, tines down, tines up, tines down. Over and over, over and over went his fork. And still he didn't speak.

"You know Willie, Dad's kid?" I said. "He said you don't want me anymore. Because you're dying."

Jake made a face. "Willie is a chicken-brained kid!" Jake said. "I never said that. I told you exactly what I told them, that I needed your dad to care for you when . . ."

He stopped, put his elbows on the table, then put his hands up to his face, his thumbs pressed into that little hollow between his eyes.

"Look," he said. "I'm an old man. My health stinks. My lungs stink. I got scared one day. I can't leave you uncared for. I had to make arrangements for you. Thing is, I never thought it would go this far."

"This far?" I said.

Jake rubbed his thumbs hard into his eyes. He was going to poke his eyes out if he didn't stop that.

"Yeah. Meaning you might really go," he said quietly.

"Do I have to?" I asked.

"Stupid question," he answered. And then he took

148

his thumbs out of his eyes and looked right at me. "But if you stay, what will happen to you after I'm gone?"

"I don't know!" I said. I couldn't bear this feeling! Couldn't bear the tears filling my eyes. "But you're . . . you're not . . . not 'going' yet, are you?"

He shook his head no. "No. No, I'm not going yet. But plan. We got to make plans."

"We did. They're done," I said. "Aren't they? If . . . if that happens, *then* I can go."

He just kept looking at me.

"It's not just for after I'm gone," he said quietly. "See, it's your dad. I was feeling that I was doing wrong by you. A girl needs that home, that security. Once we knew where your dad was, I had an obligation to you to let you go and live with him."

He smiled at me, kind of a sad smile. "I knew what you were thinking when you said that time about Parents' Night, about having your dad here for Parents' Night. Sure, it bothered me at first, when you first said that. But I got to thinking, you're right. A girl needs real family."

"Jake?" I said. "Remember the other night, the night I got back from his house? I was awake when you were in my room that night."

Jake was looking at me, eyebrows raised, that questioning look like he'd been doing the last few days.

"Well," I said, "what I realized that night is about family. You're my family."

"Your dad is family, too," Jake said.

"I know," I said. I took a deep breath, wondering if I could find the right words. "But you know my dad, how he was always saying, 'Take care of my girl'?"

Jake nodded.

Could I make him understand, understand what I found out that night?

"Well, see," I said. "What I found out is that family, *real* family, is the person who does that. You."

Suddenly I saw that Jake's eyes were wet.

He cleared his throat and looked away. "Yes," he said. "Yes."

Then quickly he got up and left the table, moving faster than I'd seen him in a long time.

I watched him head for the bathroom.

Was he sick?

He slammed the bathroom door, and in a minute, I heard the water running in the sink.

It ran for a long time.

I knew what he was doing! I do that, too, when I cry, run the water in the sink so no one will hear me.

But he couldn't be crying, not Jake!

He was, though. I'd bet anything. And I thought I knew why, too. They weren't sad tears, but the other kind, the kind you cry when you can't say what you wish you could say.

I felt tears welling up in my own eyes. I kept sitting there at the table, and after a long while, when I couldn't stand it anymore — I went to the bathroom door and stood outside it.

"Jake?" I called softly.

No answer.

"Jake? You all right?"

Still no answer, but after a moment, he yelled, "Gotta go, for Pete's sake!"

Suddenly I heard the toilet flush. Then the door opened, and Jake came out. "Can't even go to the bathroom in peace," he grumbled, brushing past me.

I couldn't help smiling. Everything was back to normal.

Chapter 18

Finally it was Parents' Night, and I couldn't believe it — even I was excited about it. I hated to admit it, but Michele had had a good idea. For once.

I had told Danielle no thanks about going with her family, that Jake and I would go alone and meet her there.

Yeah, she had a great family. But I did, too. I had Jake.

I also had a dad. But he hadn't come back to see me again, not yet. He'd called a few times, and I knew where he was if I wanted him, but I didn't want him at Parents' Night. It did feel stinky, though, that he hadn't bothered to come back at all. He kept saying he would, but so far, he hadn't. Still, it was Parents' Night. And I had Jake.

Only thing was, everybody in school had been coming down with the flu. Even Fishface had been out for most of a week — not that I missed him! — but it had delayed us getting our projects set up. Finally, though, the classroom was set up and we had all brought in our projects.

I had brought in my worm box. And I had *lots* of worms. I knew the little kid visitors to the classroom would love seeing them crawling in and out. And the sign on the box told how the worms were multiplying and were making all that rich soil. I didn't even care if the two Jasons acted like jerks about that.

Parents' Night was organized this way: All the parents would visit the different classrooms and see the kids' projects. And then we'd meet in the gym for an assembly and some speeches — Michele was going to make a speech, and I wondered what that would be like! And then there would be the food part.

The food part was the best. Jake had even donated some baked goods: muffins. I had to insist that he not put onions in them, and he agreed. Still, when we were walking to school, I secretly sniffed at them, just to be sure.

When we got to school that night, the whole building was all lit up and people were streaming in and out and I raced to my room, Jake trailing along behind looking at all the projects in the halls.

As we stopped at a bulletin board just outside the classroom, Fishface suddenly appeared, popping out of the classroom like a jack-in-the-box.

Uh-oh.

But all he did was hold out his hand to Jake. "Mr. Brady!" he said. "Nice to see you again."

Jake shook hands with him, and I noticed Jake smiling, a real kind of smile, as if he liked Fishface. And Fishface had a real kind of smile, too.

Weird!

"Haven't seen you in a while," Fishface said. "Not since . . ."

He paused.

Not since I wrapped up his car, he meant.

There was a silence then, and both Jake and Fishface turned to me, as if it was my turn to say something.

What? What to say? And then, without even thinking, I blurted out something totally embarrassing.

"Uh, how's your car?" I said.

I could see Fishface trying not to smile. But I thought Jake seemed annoyed.

And then I said something even more embarrassing — embarrassing, but I did mean it. "Mr. McGill," I said. "I'm sorry about doing that. To your car, I mean. It was really dumb."

He nodded. "That's true," he said.

"Can I fix it or something?" I said. "Polish it? I'd like to . . . do something."

He smiled then, the same kind of smile he and Jake had just exchanged. "We'll talk," he said. "We'll figure out something. How's that?"

Well, not good. But I nodded. I did feel better. For some weird reason, I hadn't been completely happy about that whole thing. Not that he didn't deserve it because he did. Still . . .

Then I went into the classroom, and as soon as I

did, I saw Danielle there, standing by the worm box with her whole family.

Just as I came up behind them, Baby tried to reach into the box. "No, Baby!" I said, and I grabbed her arm.

She turned around and stuck her lip out at me.

I picked her up. "Want to look in?" I said. "You can look. But don't touch."

Mr. and Mrs. Godwin smiled at me. Mrs. Godwin was holding Sugar, and Mr. Godwin had Tyrone by one hand and another little kid in the other.

"Hey, Brady!" Tyrone said. "Sorry about your gerbil."

I nodded. "Yeah, me, too."

Danielle gave me a look, and I smiled and shrugged.

Danielle and I had made up. I knew it wasn't her fault. She had probably felt as bad as I did. But I was saving up my money, and I was going to buy a new gerbil as soon as I had enough. I was also going to buy one for Danielle for her birthday. Our birthdays are just two days apart, and I had asked her mom if it was all right and she had agreed. She said Danielle had kept my gerbils for so long, she might as well have her own. It was a big secret, though. Neither of us was telling Danielle till her birthday came.

Danielle whispered to me, "Put Baby down. I got to show you something."

She was holding something behind her back. "Out in the hall," she said.

I handed Baby to Mr. Godwin, and Danielle and I raced out into the hall.

As soon as we were outside, she took the thing out from behind her back and handed it to me. A box. A box wrapped like a present.

"For you," she said, smiling.

"Why? It's not my birthday."

"Open it!" she said.

I started to open it, but as I was doing it, I saw that someone else was watching — Michele. She was standing there by the classroom door, looking at Danielle and me. When she saw me look at her, she turned away and went back inside. But before she turned away, I thought I noticed that she looked sad.

Danielle noticed her, too.

"What's the matter with her?" I muttered.

"Her mom and dad got sick. They have the flu."

"You mean they're not here?" I said.

Danielle nodded.

"But that's awful!" I said. "She's been planning this for so long!"

Danielle shrugged. "The stars. I told you our luck was changing. It's going to be good for us, and bad for her from now on."

"Do you really believe that?" I said. "About the stars knowing?"

She nodded.

"No," I said. "Really?"

She shrugged and looked away. " 'Course not."

"Then why do you do it?"

"Don't know. It's fun. And anyway . . ." She shrugged again.

"Anyway, what?"

She looked at me. "You know how sometimes you can't make things turn out the way you want them to?" she said. "Like even for Michele now?"

I nodded. I sure knew about that.

"So who else to blame? Might as well blame it on the stars," she said, laughing. "Open your present."

I did — tore open the box. And inside was a slip of paper and this is what it said: "Gift certificate for one gerbil. Can be redeemed at Doug's Pet Shop any time."

"Oh, thanks!" I said. "Thanks!"

I hugged her. "You shouldn't have done this! It wasn't your fault."

"I know," she said. "It was the stars!"

We both laughed, and then it was time to go down to the gym for the speeches.

I went to find Jake, and Danielle went to find her family. And then all of us started downstairs to the gym.

But as Jake and I were going down the hall together, I saw Michele in front of us, Michele walking alone in front of us.

"Hey, Michele!" I called.

She turned to me.

"Wait up!" I said. "Want to walk downstairs with us?"

She narrowed up her eyes at me, giving me a super-suspicious look.

But I just looked back, trying to look innocent. I mean I was innocent, but still, it was hard to look that way.

I didn't blame her for being suspicious, but I was trying. "I'm sorry your parents are sick," I said when we caught up to her.

She kept that suspicious look, but then she sighed. "Yeah," she said. "After all my planning."

I thought then of what Danielle had just said — how sometimes you plan and plan, but you can't make things come out all right.

Well, sometimes.

Then I said, "Michele, do you know my grandpa?"

I thought of adding, And he's not a homeless person. But I didn't.

Jake was dressed very normally that night — a sport jacket and nice pants, and real shoes — and I hadn't even had to tell him.

Michele looked at Jake, and her face got that super-fake, super-friendly look she gets when she talks to grownups.

She put out her hand. "Hello," she said.

"Hello, Michele," Jake said. "Nice plan you had here. For Parents' Night."

"Thank you!" Michele said. She smiled so hard I thought her face would split, and then she did that blinky-eye thing she does. "Got to go now!" she said. "I'm supposed to give a speech."

She ran ahead, and when she had gone, Jake looked at me. "She seems okay," he said. He frowned then and shrugged. "Twinkly, though," he said.

I shrugged, too.

"She had a good plan, anyway," I said.

"Parents' Night?" he said.

158

I nodded.

And then I thought, If it had been up to me, I wouldn't have called it Parents' Night. I'd have called it Family Night.

But then I had another thought, one that made me smile, and I actually slipped my arm through Jake's as we made our way into the gym. It really didn't matter what we called this night, I thought. We could call it anything.

What mattered was that it was a special night, one to share with family.

What mattered most was that Jake was family. And even if he had decided to wear his high-tops — or bring onion muffins — he was still real family for me.